To Have and to Hold™

SWEET NOTHINGS

CHARLOTTE HINES

SECOND CHANCE AT LOVE
BOOK

Second Chance at Love books by
Charlotte Hines

THE EARL'S FANCY   #93
TENDER TRAP   #160

SWEET NOTHINGS

First edition published October 1984

First printing

"Second Chance at Love," the butterfly emblem, and "To Have and
to Hold" are trademarks belonging to Jove Publications, Inc.

Printed in the United States of America

To Have and to Hold books are published by
The Berkley Publishing Group
200 Madison Avenue, New York, NY 10016

To F. W.
The quintessential hero

1

"LIZ LANGDON! WHAT brings you down to the hospital? Nothing's wrong, is it?"

"No, Sara." Liz smiled affectionately at the plump little woman who looked so unlike the respected professional she was. "I'm just taking a shortcut to the Medical Arts Building. I thought I'd see if I could coerce that handsome husband of mine into letting me take him out to lunch."

"How is Rochester's most distinguished pediatrician these days?" Sara fell into step with Liz.

"Busy." Liz grimaced. "Even busier than usual. He was called out late last night to diagnose a suspected Reye's syndrome and then again at five this morning to supervise an emergency cesarean."

"The Peters baby." Sara shook her graying head knowingly. "It was touch and go there for a while, but thanks to your husband, the baby made it. He's one damn fine doctor, Liz."

"I know." Liz beamed with pride. "Every time I start wishing he were a plumber or an electrician or anything that would let him stay home evenings, I meet some mother who tells me that without John her baby wouldn't be here, and I feel like the most selfish heel alive."

"Things that bad?" Sara sympathized.

"Worse." The truth slipped out. "We never seem to have any time together anymore. The phone rings constantly. Thank God I at least have the twins to keep me busy."

"Speaking of the twins, where are Jaimie and Rob?"

"In school. Today is their first day in the first grade, and I feel like crying." Liz laughed self-deprecatingly. "I always thought that once I got them into school full time I'd be delighted to have all those hours to do exactly as I pleased, but it isn't working out that way. This morning after I saw them off and went back into that empty house, I felt lost. The day suddenly seemed endless."

"The empty nest syndrome." The psychiatrist in Sara emerged briefly. "Don't worry, you'll quickly adjust."

"I'll have to. Somehow I doubt the authorities would like it much if I kept the boys out of school because I was lonely without them. At any rate, over my fifth cup of coffee I suddenly remembered how John and I often used to meet for lunch before I got tied down with the boys and he became so busy with his practice. So I decided to see if I can lure him down to Sibley's today."

"If he has the time," Sara said doubtfully. "I went past his office at ten, and it was full of whining, shrieking kids. It was like a zoo in there."

"I called his receptionist half an hour ago, and she said he had only two patients left to see, and then he'd be free until one-thirty."

"Well, if she miscalculated and he's still tied up, come down to my office. I'll give you a cup of coffee and half my peanut butter, banana, and Marshmallow Fluff sandwich," Sara offered.

"Yuck, that sounds disgusting!" Liz wrinkled her upturned nose.

"You just have plebian taste buds," Sara said with a laugh as she continued down the wide hallway of the Medical Arts Building, leaving Liz standing in front of her husband's office.

JOHN LANGDON, M.D., F.A.A.P., read the shiny brass door plaque. She sighed, remembering the day it had been mounted. John had tried so hard to act nonchalant about it, while she had been bursting with pride. All the years of studying and doing without had suddenly seemed worthwhile when she read the promise the nameplate held. John had finally achieved his goal, and she'd helped him do it. But now, older and infinitely wiser, she knew it hadn't been solely a promise the plaque held, but also a threat. It was a tangible symbol of the vast amounts of time and energy John poured into his career. A career that at times seemed to Liz's jaundiced viewpoint to be taking him over body and soul to the total exclusion of her and the twins.

Not now, she pulled herself up. Don't spoil lunch by brooding. She'd known how John felt about medicine when she married him, she reminded herself, stiffening her resolve. She knew she'd have to take second place to a very demanding profession. The trouble was, she hadn't expected second place to be so far from first. She had known that John's patients would always take precedence over her and the boys, but she hadn't expected that fact to hurt more with each passing year.

Firmly banishing her unhappy thoughts, Liz opened the door, frowning slightly at the tacky feel of the knob, no doubt due to some small patient's sticky hands.

A quick glance around the waiting room showed that for once her prayers had been answered. It was empty, and the blessed quiet held out the possibility of a pleasant lunch.

Liz made her way quietly down the hallway, the soft sound of her footsteps swallowed up by the thick beige carpeting. A smile teased her lips as she anticipated John's surprise at seeing her. She hadn't been in his office on a weekday since the twins were born six years ago.

The door to John's office was partly open, and Liz stuck her head around it, the loving greeting dying on her lips as her stunned eyes took in the scene in front of her.

A tiny blonde in a white uniform was nestled against the muscular width of John's broad chest. His six-foot frame was bent protectively over her, his powerful arms holding her securely against his white coat as she sniffed daintily into his maroon silk tie.

Liz watched in frozen disbelief as one of the blonde's small hands gently patted his masculine cheek before traveling upward to brush back the ebony strands of his hair.

As if by telepathy, Liz's fingertips vicariously felt the silkiness of his hair and the faintly raspy texture of his clean-shaven cheeks. Her palms tingled as, unbidden, her mind rushed to supply the remembered feeling of his taut, healthy skin stretched like highly polished leather over the framework of his strong bones and powerful sinews.

A wave of fury washed over her that this—this painted doll should dare to touch her husband. Liz's stomach churned, and her heart began to pound, but before her sense of betrayal could erupt into a furious accusation, the blonde's soft, babyish voice filled the air.

"Oh, Johnnie," the woman breathed, "it's so awful."

Johnnie! Liz's mind registered incredulously. He hated to be called Johnnie.

As if the blonde's words had released Liz from a spell, she stepped back out of sight. Instinct carried her out of the office and down the hall to Sara. She had no thought in her mind but that she had to escape before Johnnie—the name bit like acid into her numbed senses—and the blonde saw her.

"Liz!" Sara looked up from her conversation with her receptionist and frowned in concern. "What's wrong? You're as white as a sheet, and you're shaking. Where's John?"

"You mean Johnnie?" Liz followed Sara into her cluttered inner office, accepted a cup of coffee, and then sank down into a soft leather chair.

"Johnnie?" Sara repeated, puzzled. "Liz, what's going on?"

Liz expelled her breath in a long sigh and pressed her quivering lips together. It seemed faintly disloyal to reveal what she'd seen, but she desperately needed to talk to someone. And Sara was not just her friend; she was also a psychiatrist, which meant she was trained to deal objectively with emotional situations.

"I wish I knew." Liz sipped the scalding coffee,

scarcely noticing how hot it was.

"Why don't you start at the beginning?" Sara leaned back in her chair, giving Liz a look that combined professional interest with friendly concern. "I left you not five minutes ago all set to sample the fleshpots of downtown Rochester, and now you look like a ghost."

"I wanted to surprise John, so I didn't announce myself. I just went back to his office. Instead, I was the one who got the surprise. He was hugging a pint-sized blonde. *Bleached* blonde," Liz added acidly, "and not very expertly done at that. She called him Johnnie in a breathy little voice that made me want to give her some exercises to build up her lung capacity. How could he, Sara?" Her voice wavered.

"Do you think he's having an affair?" Sara asked calmly.

"No," Liz instinctively denied. "No!" she repeated more firmly. "John's an honorable man. If he were in love with another woman, he'd ask for a divorce. He'd never sneak around behind my back in some sordid little affair. Besides"—Liz's voice took on a tinge of bitterness—"he doesn't even have enough time for a wife, let alone a wife *and* a mistress. But who is she? I've never seen her before."

"That I can answer," Sara unexpectedly offered. "Her name's Brandy Rome. She's a student in the hospital's training program for medical secretaries. They serve a two-month stint in a doctor's office at the end of their course."

"Oh, then, it's educational," Liz sniped. "That explains it all."

"Actually, John is Brandy's second assignment," Sara said, ignoring the interruption. "Her first was with an obstetrician. Apparently she threw herself body and soul into pleasing him, and his wife took exception to the 'body' part. So Brandy was transferred."

"Great, a femme fatale!"

"Not exactly." Sara seemed to be weighing her words, and Liz looked at her impatiently.

"Come on, Sara, spill it. You know as well as I do that this hospital's like a small town. You might as well tell me, because I can easily find out. There's always someone brimming over with eagerness to repeat the latest gossip."

"All right," Sara sighed, sinking back into her chair. "According to my receptionist, Brandy makes no secret of the fact that she entered the medical field for the express purpose of finding a doctor for a husband. The fact that her original choice already had a wife she regarded as no more than a minor inconvenience. Her only miscalculation with the obstetrician was in assuming that he meant to divorce his wife and marry her."

"Good God, she couldn't be dumb enough to equate sex with commitment, could she?"

"Who knows what she thinks, or even if she does?" Sara shrugged. "I've never had much to do with her. But I know that when it came time to reassign her, none of the other doctors would take her. Even though the administration tried to hush up the incident, the obstetrician's wife was too vocal for it not to leak out."

"So John offered," Liz stated fatalistically, knowing her husband's propensity for helping stray lambs. Although Brandy Rome struck her as more piranha than lamb.

"That's about the extent of it," Sara agreed. "But I'm sure he's not having an affair with her."

"At least not yet," Liz said thoughtfully.

"What's that supposed to mean?"

"I'm not sure, exactly." Liz ran trembling fingers through her shoulder-length brown hair. "Maybe I've been reading too many magazine articles about men going off the rails when they reach their forties and trying to recapture their youth with a much younger woman. John will be forty in November, and God knows that blond bombshell is a lot younger than my thirty-five. She must be about the same age I was when I married John."

"What's the matter with you, Liz? You're a level-headed, rational woman. It isn't like you to go to pieces over what was probably an isolated incident."

"Maybe it is, and maybe it isn't." Liz shook her head uncertainly. "But seeing him holding another woman seemed to bring things into focus, and I don't like the picture one little bit."

"Oh, come on," Sara scoffed. "John is the least likely candidate for an attack of male menopause that I can think of."

"Perhaps, but I'd also have been willing to bet that I'd never find him hugging his secretary either," Liz pointed out. "Maybe I am overreacting, but this just fits the classic pattern too perfectly. John's exhibiting all the symptoms of a man who's bored with his marriage. He's always busy with his work, to the exclusion of his wife and family. We never seem to talk anymore; I mean really talk, about our feelings, our hopes, about anything that matters. I'm lucky if I even *see* him in the evening, let alone hold a meaningful discussion with him. And add to all that the presence of another woman on the scene." Liz shrugged despondently. "I don't for a minute believe he's cheating on me, but everything I've read makes me suspect that he's ripe for an affair." She paused. "I don't think I could bear it, Sara," she said flatly. "If possible, I love John more than I did fifteen years ago when we got married, and yet he seems to be slipping farther away from me every day."

"So *do* something about it. The first step in solving a problem is to identify it, and you've just done that. You say he's bored, so add some interest to your marriage."

"You make me sound like a one-woman variety show." Liz smiled involuntarily. "But it isn't that simple. For one thing, considering the amount of time he spends at home, I doubt he'd notice no matter what I tried. Then again, some things are beyond my control. Take Blondie, for example. What do I do about her?"

"You could demand that he have her transferred," Sara suggested.

"No." Liz shook her head. "That would be tantamount to saying I didn't trust him. Besides which, it would be embarrassing for him to have to tell the director of the training school that his wife wanted his secretary transferred. I couldn't do that to his pride."

"Then what are you going to do?"

"Right now I'm going to march back to his office, pry that unscrupulous little man-eater away from him, and take him out to lunch. After that"—Liz's voice momentarily sounded bleak—"after that, I don't know."

John's waiting room was still empty, but this time Liz made no attempt to go back to her husband's office. Instead, she called out, "Hello, is anyone here?"

Her query was answered almost immediately by Brandy, who emerged from the supply closet behind the receptionist's desk.

"It's lunchtime, and the doctor isn't here." She frowned at Liz. "He won't be back until one-thirty."

Liz bit down her annoyance at the woman's summary dismissal, telling herself not to be overly sensitive. "I know it's lunchtime," she began, but before she could continue John came out of his office at the end of the hall.

"Liz!" The pleasure in his voice and the warm welcome in his night-dark eyes did a great deal to soothe her fevered imaginings. Whatever his feelings about their marriage, at this moment he really was glad to see her.

"What are you doing downtown? Are Rob and Jaimie here, too?" He glanced around as if expecting to find the boys under the furniture.

"Today's the first day of school," Liz reminded him, not the least surprised that he'd forgotten. The way he was pushing himself lately, it was a wonder he remembered what month it was, let alone the date. "And since I didn't have the boys underfoot, I decided to treat you to lunch."

Brandy rushed into speech. "Oh, but we've already ordered sandwiches."

"Then I bequeath you Dr. Langdon's sandwich, Miss . . . ?" Liz forced a polite smile. Although she wanted to tell Brandy Rome to get lost, Liz was smart enough to know she'd get a lot further by appearing to be sweetly reasonable. John hated catty females, and if he really had adopted Blondie as one of his stray lambs, he'd be quick to defend her.

"Rome, Brandy Rome," John supplied. "She's interning with us for a couple of months. Brandy, this is my wife, Liz."

"Brandy." Liz nodded politely, just as if Sara had not forewarned her.

"Mrs. Langdon." Brandy's exaggeratedly respectful demeanor was clearly intended to put Liz in another generation. More annoying to Liz was Brandy's failure to excuse herself and leave them to talk in private.

"Let's go, John. We've got an hour and fifteen minutes left," Liz urged him.

"Oh, but . . ." Brandy tried again, but John ignored her. He slipped out of his lab coat and grabbed his gray wool suit jacket.

"That's the best offer I've had today." His handsome face creased in a smile. "I just hope you've got more than my thirty-two cents, because I'm starved."

"No, but I have one of your credit cards," Liz said with a chuckle.

"You're on." John took her arm as he guided her out the door.

"Good-bye, Brandy. Nice to meet you." Liz smiled blandly into the girl's frustrated features, almost feeling sorry for her. Brandy was so transparent as to be pathetic.

"Let me drive," Liz suggested as they walked through the doctors' parking lot toward her dark green station wagon. "You can sit back and relax until we get there."

"Relax! With you driving?" he protested as he got into the passenger's side.

"Hah! Male chauvinist. You know perfectly well that I haven't had an accident yet."

"It's the *yet* that worries me." He leaned back against the headrest, closed his eyes, and rubbed the bridge of his nose with his lean fingers.

Liz slipped behind the wheel and turned to look at him. A wave of tenderness at his obvious weariness washed over her. He looked every one of his thirty-nine years and then some.

"Tired?" she asked softly.

"Mmm," he sighed, "but good tired. The emergency last night wasn't Reye's syndrome, the Peters baby is out of the woods, and, with any luck at all, I should get home for dinner tonight. I'm going to sit back, put my feet up, and watch the football game on TV."

"Yes, Grampa." Liz leaned against his relaxed body to grab his shoulder harness, but as her breasts brushed across the firm wall of his chest, the thought of buckling him in slipped from her mind. A tingling sensation spread from the slight contact, and she deliberately relaxed into him, letting his body support her. She absorbed the feel of his breath catching, but other than that he remained passive, his body relaxed, his eyes closed.

Liz studied him, then smiled to herself. Unaffected, was he? She'd see how long he could stay that way. She hadn't been married to him for fifteen years without learning a thing or two about what turned him on.

Slowly she traced his left ear with her fingertip, then slipped lower to gently scrape the tip of her nail over his firm jawline. The scratchy feel of her nail on his emerging beard vibrated through her arm, raising a slight shiver of awareness.

Encouraged by the way his breathing deepened, Liz pulled herself up, deliberately rubbing her breasts against his chest as she slowly moved up and down.

Drawing satisfaction from the involuntary gasp that escaped his parted lips, she turned her attention to his right ear.

Tentatively the tip of her tongue darted out to explore it in a series of devastating forays. The heady scent of his spicy after shave filled her nostrils as the faintly salty taste of his skin filled her mouth.

"Liz, what are you doing?"

"And you have a degree in medicine?" she absently teased him, more interested in the taste and feel of him than in what he was saying. Her eyelids slid shut, the better to concentrate on her body's reaction to him. Her lips left his ear to drop a series of butterfly kisses along his jaw and then down toward his mouth.

"It's broad daylight, and we're in a very open parking lot near a very respectable hospital in Rochester, New York," John protested halfheartedly as his hands closed around her body, lifting her onto his lap.

Liz wiggled her trim hips on his hard thighs in a deliberately provocative move as she studied his firm lips with eager anticipation.

"God, you're a witch," he whispered hoarsely, his hardening body leaving her in no doubt of his reaction to her advances.

"Johnnie? Oh!" came a wispy voice through the side window.

"Oh, hell," Liz sighed, slumping into John's chest as Brandy's words interrupted them.

"What are you doing?" Brandy blurted out as she peered in the open window.

"What is it with people in the medical profession?" Liz addressed the car roof. "Not a one of them seems to know anything about sex."

"I don't know about her, but I intend to explore

the concept more fully during halftime tonight." John's body shook with laughter.

"It's nice to know where I fit into your priorities," Liz said tartly.

"It's so public here," Brandy objected, obviously unnerved by the sight of Liz snuggled into John's lap.

"He couldn't help it. I flung myself at him and wouldn't let go." Liz smiled knowingly, taking a great deal of satisfaction from the wary look that suddenly flashed in Brandy's china-blue eyes. "What can we do for you?" Liz started to slip off John's lap, but his arms tightened, holding her still.

"Don't move," he whispered in her ear. "We don't want to shock the poor kid with the facts of life."

"Hmm." Liz couldn't resist a grin at his dilemma even though she was willing to give him odds that Brandy could outlast him shock for shock.

"What is it, Brandy?" His voice became incisive, losing its teasing quality.

"Mrs. Farber called and said her kid's sick, and I don't know what to do."

"What's the matter specifically?" John asked.

"Specifically?" Brandy sounded confused.

"Brandy, we've been over this before. Is the baby running a fever? In pain? Vomiting? What are his symptoms?" Liz recognized the impatient edge in John's voice. He was fed up. It would appear Brandy was overplaying her poor-little-me act.

"Go call Mrs. Farber back. If she's still worried, squeeze her in after two. If she isn't, I'll call her myself about one-thirty. Mrs. Farber is a brand-new mother, and she tends to panic over the least thing. She probably just needs a little support from us. Now run along and take care of it."

Brandy grimaced, not even trying to hide her chagrin over being so summarily dismissed. Liz gave her a sympathetic smile, even though she was of the opinion that Brandy deserved the mild reproof John had handed out. Brandy had obviously used the phone call as an excuse to rush out to the doctors' parking lot in the hope of spoiling their lunch plans. The blonde reluctantly turned to go.

"To be continued tonight." John dropped a hard kiss on Liz's softly parted lips and then tipped her off his lap. "Drive," he playfully commanded, buckling his seat belt and leaning back. "I'm starved, and who knows what I might start to nibble on if I'm not fed quickly."

"Tempting," Liz murmured as she obediently started the station wagon, "but we must think of your position, Johnnie." The acerbic comment escaped before she could stop it.

"Don't mind Brandy." John yawned. "She's having a tough time of it lately."

And she's going to have an even tougher time of it if she doesn't learn to keep her claws off other women's husbands, Liz thought as she swung the wagon out of the lot with a jerk, eliciting a smothered protest from John.

Ten minutes later, with a deft twist of her slim wrists, she negotiated a tiny parking space.

"There! What'd I tell you?" Liz crowed triumphantly. "There was plenty of room. At least there is as long as you're willing to get out on my side."

"Is it safe to look?" John peeped through the fingers clutched over his eyes. He glanced at the pink Cadillac a scant three inches from his door handle and shuddered. "My wife, the kamikaze driver. What I can't figure out is why you've never had an accident."

"Great depth perception," she said smugly. "Come on, let's eat. I'm starved."

"So am I." He leered at her, and Liz grinned back, suddenly feeling lighthearted.

She wiggled out of the car and then squeaked when she felt two firm fingers pinch her softly rounded bottom.

"John Langdon!" She swung on him.

"Sorry." He gave her a seraphic smile. "I couldn't resist."

He watched her write down the number of the area where she'd parked. Ever since the day she managed to forget where she'd left her car, she'd been very careful.

They rode up to the shopping level on the escalator, strolled through the covered mall, then made their way across the area to Sibley's department store.

"Protect me!" Liz hissed as they made their way toward the bank of elevators.

"Protect you?" John looked startled. "From what?"

"We have to go right past the Godiva chocolates display."

"You're expecting a box of vanilla creams to grab you as you go by?"

"They don't have to," Liz said gloomily. "All they have to do is sit there, and I'll grab them."

"So what?"

"So what! Do you have any idea how many calories are in a box of chocolates? I could gain five pounds just looking at them."

"As long as you gain it in the right place." John's eyes skimmed over her slight body, lingering on the firm swell of her small breasts, and his hand moved up her arm to "accidentally" brush against her soft flesh.

Liz shivered at the sensations that tore through her.

"As a matter of fact, I think I'll help the process along." He stopped at the Godiva counter and gave the elderly woman behind it a blinding smile. "A three-pound box of assorted chocolates, please."

"John!" Liz poked him.

"I'm hurrying, darling. She has the most frightful cravings," he explained to the interested saleswoman.

"Almost homocidal!" Liz glared at him.

"I remember just how it was when I was carrying my children." The older woman smiled conspiratorially at the embarrassed Liz. "Only in my case, it was fried potatoes, of all things." She shook her head at the thought as she put the candy box into a small gold shopping bag and handed it to John.

Liz watched resignedly as John absently explored his pockets before she sighed and reached into her purse. "Here." She handed the saleswoman the small white credit card.

"Thanks, Liz. I seem to have left my wallet somewhere."

"No doubt with your car keys," she said, hazarding a guess based on fifteen years' experience.

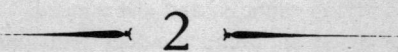

2

"Two?" THE HOSTESS asked as her interested gaze lingered on John's chiseled features in a manner that unexpectedly annoyed Liz.

"Yes." John gave the woman an impersonal smile, not seeming to notice her not-so-covert glances.

Liz shook her head as she followed the woman's trim figure across the huge crowded room. What on earth was the matter with her? It had been years since she'd noticed the way other women habitually looked at John, and now, suddenly, she was not only noticing, but objecting. Seeing Brandy in John's arms this morning had shattered the safe, secure cocoon she'd immersed herself in, and forced her to face her marriage as it was instead of as she wished it to be.

The hostess paused to make way for a young woman carrying a tiny infant and shepherding a sturdy toddler. The toddler overbalanced and plopped down on her diaper-clad rear. She opened her mouth, but before she could give vent to her frustrations, John reached

down, picked her up, and set her on her feet. The
child blinked at him in surprise, obviously intrigued
by the huge stranger.

"Dada!" she pronounced triumphantly, totally
oblivious to her mother's embarrassed gasp.

"Sorry," the woman apologized. *"Dada* is her word
of the week."

"Her father must be very proud of her."

Liz, sensitive to the nuances in John's voice, caught
the underlying sadness, and she winced.

John loved children, and they had planned on a
somewhat larger family, hoping for both boys and
girls. But the miserable time Liz had had while carrying the twins, coupled with the terror of the emergency cesarean that had brought them into the world,
had made her hesitant to risk having another child.
When the twins had turned three, John had suggested
it was a good time to add to their family, but Liz had
stalled, saying she wanted to wait until Jaimie and
Rob were well established in nursery school. Then
she'd wanted to wait until they were in kindergarten,
until finally John had ceased to ask at all.

Liz slipped her hand into his and gave it a squeeze.

John glanced down at her in surprise, and one mo-
bile eyebrow quirked upward questioningly. Liz shook
her head, uncertain even in her own mind to which
of them she was offering comfort. To John for the
loss of the daughter he'd always wanted? Or to herself
for being too cowardly to face another pregnancy?

The hostess stopped by a small table for two tucked
away behind one of the massive cream-colored pillars
that supported the lofty ceiling. She put two menus
down, smiled regretfully at John, and left.

John helped Liz into her chair before sitting down opposite her.

"What may I have?" She smiled at him, remembering the days during medical school and his residency when money had been so tight that whenever they'd eaten out she'd carefully asked beforehand just what their frail budget could handle.

"Whatever you want." His eyes lingered on the soft, pink moistness of her lips.

"And if it isn't on the menu?" Liz's eyes brimmed with amusement.

"Ah, but it's the specialty of the house," he responded with seeming seriousness. "Tonight..."

"I know," Liz sniffed, "during halftime."

"For a special customer like you I might be willing to sacrifice the first few minutes of the third quarter."

"Gee, now that's devotion." Liz widened her eyes in mock astonishment.

"May I help you?" the waitress cut into their nonsense.

"Just the salad bar and coffee for me," Liz ordered. John chose roast beef.

"Help yourself to the salad bar," the waitress instructed as she set down two steaming cups of coffee.

When John's order arrived, Liz took her plate and approached the huge circular bar where easily twenty-five different offerings were displayed. In no time at all she'd filled her dish, and she looked regretfully at the delicacies still waiting to be sampled.

"You could always ask for a doggie bag," John teased her as he added a plain lettuce salad and a roll to his pile of pink roast beef.

"Mmm." Liz barely heard him as she concentrated

on fitting a spoonful of oil-cured olives between her deviled eggs and citrus fruit salad.

"Come on, Liz, I promise to bring you back next week to try the rest of it. Especially if you're treating."

"I thought men were supposed to be sensitive about having a woman pay," she commented as they made their way back to their table.

"Ah, but it's different when you're married." He smiled at her as they sat down. "I distinctly remember hearing the priest say that we were now one person, and what was yours was mine and what was mine was mine."

"Yeah, but . . ." Liz began and then stopped as what he'd said penetrated. "Wait a minute there, friend. I think you've done a little judicious editing. That isn't the way I remember it."

"Perhaps not," John conceded. "I will admit I wasn't paying a great deal of attention to the ceremony. All I could think about was that I was going to do first when I finally got you into bed."

"John Langdon!" Liz tried to look suitably shocked but failed miserably. "Before the altar of God!"

"It's his own fault." John shrugged. "He was the one who said to go forth and multiply."

"*Go forth* was the salient phrase," Liz said with a grin. "As eager as you were, I'm surprised we made it to the motel room."

"Ah, but it wasn't my fault," he excused himself. "You were one sexy little broad."

Were! The word hit Liz with the force of a sledgehammer, and she hurriedly bent her head to hide her dismay. His use of the past tense reverberated through her mind. Staunchly she took herself not to be stupid, that it was merely a slip of the tongue. But what worried her was that it might have been a Freudian slip. Was that what he really felt deep down? That at twenty she'd been a sexy woman, but now, at thirty-five, she had lost her appeal?

"What's wrong, Liz?" John's frown of concern fed her shaky self-confidence. She was being ridiculous, she assured herself.

"Nothing." She forced a bright smile, trying hard to believe it. "I was just deliberating on what to try first."

It was obvious John didn't believe her, but to her relief he let the subject drop.

Liz was beginning to think that for once they'd make it through a meal without being interrupted when his pager emitted a shrill beep. He turned it off and smiled ruefully at her.

"Almost," he sighed.

"It's okay. I've already finished most of my coffee, and I've got the chocolates for dessert." She nodded toward the gold bag. "You go call your answering service and find out which of your charges has committed mayhem while I get the check."

"You can apply my thirty-two cents toward the total," he offered.

"It may come to that," she threatened, "if this lunch has overextended our credit." As he walked away, she smiled down at the grand tally of eleven dollars and eighty-three cents and figured a tip.

"Liz! What are you doing downtown?" A vivacious, stick-thin redhead with a plump, balding man in tow stopped by the table. "Where are the twins?"

"Good heavens, Carol, the twins and I aren't an inseparable item, you know." The question had flicked Liz's already raw nerves. "Hi, Gary," she added, nodding to Carol's husband, who was one of John's colleagues.

"It just seems that way?" Carol quipped. "Seriously, though, what are you doing here by yourself?" Her gaze slid to the empty plate across from Liz. "Or is this an assignation?" she whispered melodramatically.

"Yes." Liz glanced around, as if making sure no one could overhear her, and then murmured, "With the love of my life."

"Speaking of which . . ." Gary smiled as John approached.

"Carol, Gary," John greeted them, then dropped his hand to Liz's neck and gave it a gentle squeeze. "I'm afraid we'll have to leave now, honey. That was the emergency room."

"Nothing serious, I hope." She moved to gather up her chocolates and purse.

"No, a toddler fell into a coffee table and cut his head. He may need a few stitches, and the mother a tranquilizer. According to the nurse, she's having hysterics."

"Go ahead and finish your coffee, Liz," Gary offered. "I'm on my way back to the hospital. I'll give John a lift, and then you can go shopping with Carol."

Unwilling to trade the return trip in her husband's company for an afternoon of shopping, Liz was about to refuse when John took the decision out of her hands.

"Thanks, Gary. I wanted to talk to you about the Willings baby anyway. I'll catch up with you at the cashier."

"Fine." Gary nodded and turned away.

"I have to go to the ladies' room. Meet me there,

okay, Liz?" Carol instructed before walking off with Gary.

"Okay," Liz agreed, still uncertain she wanted to spend the afternoon trailing along behind Carol. It wasn't that she didn't like Carol. She did. They'd been friends ever since they went to kindergarten together. However, in her present disturbed state of mind, Liz knew she wasn't ready to confide in Carol, yet she wasn't sure she was up to making the effort to appear carefree either. But even less did she want to go home and listen to the deafening silence.

"Have fun this afternoon," John ordered, "and buy something for yourself instead of for the twins." He traced his forefinger lightly over the bridge of her nose and then lightly outlined her lips.

Liz's stomach contracted at the sensual caress, and she caught his finger between her teeth and lightly licked it with the tip of her tongue.

"Keep that up, love, and I may decide to forgo the football game tonight and indulge in a few games of my own."

"Rank heresy," Liz chided as she got up. "As long as I'm going shopping, can I get you anything?"

"I can't think of a thing." John guided her across the room with a possessive hand on the small of her back.

"You have everything you need for that meeting in Washington this week?"

"Convention," he corrected her. "It's the annual pediatrics convention."

"Oh." Liz wanted to tell him she could hardly be expected to know what it was, since he hadn't bothered to tell her, but honesty made her admit that in recent years she hadn't made much of an attempt to listen when he talked about his professional gatherings. Or much else for that matter, the unhappy thought intruded.

"Have an acceptable afternoon." Liz gave him a discreet peck on the cheek as he left her at the entrance to the ladies' lounge.

She found Carol stretched out on one of the stuffed sofas, muttering to herself.

"You all right?" Liz sank down across from her.

"Sure, that's my mantra. I'm gathering my energies for this afternoon."

"Mantra?" Liz frowned.

"It's a new course I'm enrolled in. Meditation. It's supposed to expand my consciousness, but I'm afraid the only thing that's expanding is my waistline. The instructor's wife bakes the most delicious pastries for coffee breaks."

"The pitfalls of higher education?"

"How would you know?" Carol playfully gibed. "I doubt you've been to a class since you dropped out of college to support John during med school."

"Education is not limited to formal instruction," Liz said mildly, too used to Carol's wayward tongue to take offense. "To be honest, I went to college in the first place only because I didn't know what I wanted to do with my life. Once I met John, I did." Liz's lips twitched at Carol's disgusted expression.

"That's degrading!" Carol sniffed. "You need to find fulfillment."

"If mumbling *'oh mani padme'* is fulfillment, forget it. And if you don't lay off the liberated-woman spiel, you can forget me, too. I already have the twins. I don't need any more aggravation."

"Aggravation!" Carol's finely plucked eyebrows arched upward. "You refer to the sacred state of motherhood as aggravation?"

"I'm warning you, Carol."

"Sorry," Carol laughed, "I couldn't resist. Normally you're so wrapped up in the twins that to hear you actually admit that motherhood isn't all peaches and cream comes as a bit of a shock."

"Is that how I seem to you?" Liz asked uneasily. "Totally immersed in motherhood?"

"I didn't mean it nastily," Carol replied uncertainly. "It's just that you never go to conventions or meetings like the rest of us."

"Well, things should get better with the twins in school full time. Now, what's on your agenda this afternoon? I've got an hour and a half to kill. We dedicated mother types are always home to meet the school bus." Liz's words were light, but inwardly Carol's statements had been curiously unsettling. She had no desire to be known as a supermom who doted on her children at the expense of her husband. Had she really been neglecting John in favor of the twins? Her earlier misgivings returned full force, but she determinedly shook them off.

"First I want to visit the book department, and then lingerie. Gary's taking me to Washington with him this weekend, and I want something sexy to wear."

"Lucky you." Liz suppressed an unexpected flash of envy at Carol's childless state, which made it possible for her to accompany her husband on almost all his business trips.

The book department was a mass of women of all ages, sizes, and descriptions. Liz looked around in disbelief at the jostling humanity.

"What on earth is going on?" she asked Carol. "I haven't seen this many women jockeying for position since that baseball player who models underwear came here to sign autographs in the men's department two years ago."

"Yeah." Carol's eyes took on a faraway gleam. "I still have the briefs he signed. Remember?"

"Remember! One does not forget a friend who shoves a pair of shorts at a man, asks him to sign them, and then blurts out that he looks much better in his underwear than her husband does."

"So I got flustered," Carol blithely excused herself. "I didn't know he was going to be there, and all I had for him to sign were the shorts I'd just bought. There was no call for you to rush off as if you didn't know me."

"Never mind that," Liz dismissed her defection. "Who's here today?"

"Bliss Storm." Carol breathed the name in a reverent tone.

"Storm . . . Storm . . ." Liz frowned thoughtfully. "What's she written?"

"What's she written!" Carol looked at her, scandalized. "For your information, my illiterate friend, Bliss Storm just happens to be the hottest author going. Why, her *Passion in the Sand* was at the top of the best-seller list for ages."

"Sounds uncomfortable."

"Sounds like fun, you mean." Carol sighed enviously. "She's been on all the talk shows and—"

"No, not that," Liz interrupted. "I meant passion in the sand sounds uncomfortable. All those gritty little grains in your hair and on your skin. To say nothing of the prickly plants and the bugs or—"

"Liz Langdon, you have no romance in your soul!"

"Why do you say that? Because I prefer a nice comfortable bed to the sandy ground?"

"Beds are boring." Carol threw her hands into the air. "I mean, anyone can use a bed. What a relationship needs is an element of excitement, of danger."

"I could get that by seducing my husband on his examining table," Liz teased. "Those things are hard as a rock, narrow, and well off the ground. I don't have to find a sandbox."

"You're hopeless! How you've ever managed to hang on to a gorgeous hunk like John with your conventional ideas is a mystery to me," Carol retorted, not noticing when Liz paled at her words. "Stay here while I get in line for my autographed copy."

Liz nodded, not trusting her voice. Carol's thorough if thoughtless denunciation was serving to reinforce her own assessment of the perilous state of her marriage. She wasn't hidebound, was she? Simply because she didn't have the slightest desire to play slap-and-tickle in the sand with some latter-day sheikh of Araby? But was there a kernel of truth in Carol's careless condemnation?

Liz stared blindly at a display of cookbooks. Had she allowed their lovemaking to slip into a rut, even though she found it a satisfying rut? After fifteen years, was John bored with her? Did he yearn for a reckless young heroine who'd be thrilled to cavort in the sands? Was that what Brandy's attraction was— assuming he really was attracted?

"May I help you, madam?" The polite voice of the saleswoman cut into Liz's unhappy thoughts, and she turned toward the elderly face.

"No, thank you." Liz forced a smile. "I'm just

waiting for my friend to get Miss Storm's autograph. From the looks of things, it'll be a while."

"Yes." The woman smiled with pride. "The signing is turning out to be quite a success, if I do say so myself. Miss Storm writes such wonderful books, although I definitely think *Passion in the Sand* is her best to date. Don't you?"

Liz was saved the necessity of answering when the woman suddenly moved off to intervene as a customer tried to break into line.

Liz took the opportunity to slip around a bookcase, out of sight of the crowd. She was browsing through a section of self-help books when her eye was caught by a large cardboard display adorned with a life-sized blowup of a voluptuous-looking woman in the arms of a handsome man whose physique would have put Tarzan to shame. Under the picture, printed in bold black letters, was the question DOES YOUR HUSBAND SWEEP YOU OFF YOUR FEET?

"No," Liz muttered to herself. "My husband would probably make a crack about setting himself up as a prime candidate for a hernia." Curious, she picked up one of the books in the display. The same overmuscled man and underdressed woman were depicted on the cover below the title *Ten Foolproof Ways to Invigorate a Tired Marriage*.

Intrigued, Liz opened the book and began to read the preface. She frowned as the author exhorted her readers to use the methods outlined in the book to protect their husbands from the dangers of middle age, when many wives—presumably those without the information contained in these chapters—would lose their men to younger women. Turning to the table of contents, Liz skimmed it with interest, noting chapters about competing with a younger woman, meeting a man on his own intellectual plane, and adding spice to a routine sex life.

Liz closed the book and took a furtive glance around, feeling much as she had back in junior high when she stole a peek inside a *Playboy* magazine. She'd always thought she had such a perfect marriage. Everyone always told her that. But now, in the course of one morning, she seemed to be foundering in a sea of uncertainty, and this book promised to guide her through the confusing depths. Making up her mind, Liz dug her charge card out of her purse and headed toward the friendly saleswoman. The ideas in the book might not work, but then again, they might. At the very least, reading it might serve to crystallize the doubts filling her mind.

"God!" Carol gasped as she reached Liz fifteen minutes later, her autographed book clutched triumphantly to her chest. "Women can be such bitches! One of them actually stabbed me in the back with an umbrella when I tried to talk to Storm about her new book." She noted Liz's bag. "Oh, you bought something, too. Let me guess. Something for the twins, right?"

"Right," Liz lied, knowing that if Carol had any inkling of what she'd really bought, she'd never hear the end of it.

"Really, Liz, you're hopelessly suburban," Carol mourned. "Ignoring Bliss Storm in favor of a kid's book!"

"At least I didn't get poked in the back." Liz pointed out.

"It was worth it. Now, then," Carol said, reverting to her usually brisk self, "we'd best get up to lingerie if you have to be home by two-thirty."

Liz trailed along behind Carol as they crossed the wide expanse of gray carpeting that led into the intimate apparel department. She glanced around at the racks full of silky slips, scraps of lace panties and matching bras, and seductive chiffon nightgowns. They were worlds away from her customary fare of plain white bras, cotton briefs, and bright flannel pajamas.

"What exactly are you looking for, Carol?"

"Something that'll knock my husband's socks off. To say nothing of the rest of his clothes. He may be at meetings all day, but I fully intend to occupy his nights. Hmm." She paused to examine some baby-doll pajamas. "What do you think?"

"If they charge by the square inch, you can get them for under a dollar," Liz teased, "even at today's inflated prices."

"Why don't you go to the pediatrics convention with John?" Carol lost interest in the outfit. "I should think you'd want to hear him."

"Hear him?"

"Give the keynote address," Carol said impatiently. "It's really quite an honor to be asked, you know. Gary would have given his eyeteeth for the privilege."

"Oh?" Liz turned and pretended to be studying a flannel nightgown so Carol couldn't see the shock her words had caused. John had been paid the singular honor of being asked to give the keynote address, and he hadn't even bothered to tell her—let alone ask her to come and hear him. As a matter of fact, he hadn't asked her to accompany him to one of these affairs since the time he was invited to read a research paper, and that was almost five years ago. He'd been an excited bundle of nerves, she remembered. She'd fully intended to go with him to give him moral support, but at the last minute one of the twins had grown fussy, and she'd been unable to desert him. So she'd begged off, reasoning that at their tender age the twins needed her more than a grown man did.

Now for the first time she began to wonder at the wisdom of that decision. Maybe she should have steeled herself to leave, knowing that the twins would be well cared for. Maybe if she had, she wouldn't now be in the position of finding out about her husband's accomplishments from the wife of one of his colleagues.

A flash of panic shook her as the full import of just how isolated from her husband's interests she'd become over the years. It hadn't always been that way. In the beginning John had shared all his day-to-day triumphs as well as the defeats with her. Before the twins. Before both their days had seemingly become too full to handle all the demands on their time. Somehow, one of the first things to go had been the long conversations they'd once had.

What had happened? she wondered. Had John found a more sympathetic ear than hers? The image of Brandy Rome flashed through her mind, and her grip tightened on her book as if it were a talisman that could ward off predatory women.

"Liz!" The impatience in Carol's voice shook Liz free from her disquieting thoughts. "What on earth is the matter with you? You're staring at that hideous nightie as if it were a physical threat."

"Sorry." Liz took a deep breath and glanced at a rack of pure silk panties. Men were supposed to like seductive lingerie, weren't they? As a matter of fact, she'd be willing to bet that the book she'd just bought contained a whole chapter on seductive underwear.

"You know, Carol, I feel very reckless all of a sudden."

"Ha!" Carol scoffed. "What are you going to do? Buy flowered pajamas instead of plain ones?"

"Nope. I intend to buy a whole new wardrobe of sexy lingerie. You can help me choose, if you want to."

"Are you serious?" Carol looked dumbfounded. "Somehow you just don't seem like the sexy type. You're much more the girl next door. You know, like Doris Day."

"At least she always got her man."

"You've already got a man," Carol pointed out. "And what a man. If I weren't madly in love with my own little balding, potbellied darling, I'd envy you."

"You would?" Liz asked uncertainly. In all the years she'd known Carol, she'd never realized that John appealed to her.

"Honey, I'd have to be blind not to be aware of his attributes, and I don't mean just physical. Your husband is one helluva nice guy."

"Thanks." Liz smiled weakly, Carol's tribute adding to her mushrooming unease. It was one thing for Liz to think her own husband was a sexy man, but to have her friend come right out and admit it was disquieting. It was just one more thing she'd been hit with today. Mentally she winced. If someone had told her this morning that her innocent impulse to have lunch with her husband would plunge her calm, well-ordered life into a seething caldron of confused uncertainty, she would have laughed at the idea.

But had her life really been all that calm and placid? Liz wondered. Or had all that calmness really been only a thin layer of ice, beneath which myriad unacknowledged and unresolved problems lay. Her preoccupation with the twins and John's increasing submersion in his work hadn't happened overnight. Had what she'd seen in John's office this morning been a stone that served to break the icy calmness and allow the problems to force their way to the surface? She didn't know, but one thing she was sure of: The steady ebb and flow of her existence had been irrevocably destroyed.

3

"FIRST GRADE'S AB...SO...LUTE...LY super, Mom." Jaimie stopped rhapsodizing just long enough to shove yet another chocolate chip cookie into his mouth.

Rob, taking advantage of Jaimie's temporary inability to talk, rushed into speech. "It really is, Mom. We sat in the back of the bus with the big boys, and one of them showed us how to make the bestest spitballs."

"Spitballs!" Liz frowned.

"Yeah." Jaimie gulped down his cookie and took up the narrative. "You have to chew 'em first. That's what makes 'em all hard, and then they go real far."

"Real far." Rob's ebony eyes gleamed with remembered pleasure. "I threw one five seats up," he bragged. "It hit that dumb Ellie Kaminsky right in the back of the neck."

"It went splat!" Jaimie made a descriptive sound, managing to spray cookie crumbs all over the kitchen table.

"She screamed. Real loud," Rob added with ghoulish satisfaction.

"The bus driver did, too."

"You didn't hit Mrs. Dickson, did you?" Liz demanded.

"Oh, no." Rob's face was the picture of angelic innocence. "I wouldn't do that. You said never to distract the driver."

"Well, listen up, you two, because I'm about to say something else." Liz pinned her two offspring with a compelling stare. "You are never, ever, to make or use a spitball. Under any circumstances," she added when she saw the calculating gleam in Rob's eye.

"But, Mom," Jaimie protested, "we only spit them at girls. Not at real people."

"I'll have you know that *I'm* a girl."

"No, you're not!" Rob seemed outraged by her claim. "You're a mom, and moms are too old to be girls. Girls are all wet."

"It's no wonder, what with you throwing spitballs all over the poor things."

"But Mom . . ."

"But nothing. I mean it." Liz suppressed the impulse to threaten to tell their father about their exploits. She had never given in to the urge to use John as a bogeyman to scare the twins into obeying her. Instead, she handled discipline herself as the need arose, knowing that at their age, punishment had to be meted out promptly after the deed. It couldn't wait until John came home; by then the boys probably would have forgotten what they were being punished for. But just once she would like to have John there to share the unpleasant burden of discipline.

"Do you understand?" Past experience with the

boys' ability to obey the letter of the law while ignoring the spirit had made her leery of leaving a subject until they had thoroughly discussed it.

"How about outside?" Rob, always the last to give up, bargained.

"No spitballs in any way, shape, or form. Anywhere, anytime. Understand?"

"Yeah, but I don't like it," Rob protested.

"Jaimie?" Liz immediately regretted asking when he opened his mouth to speak and displayed an enormous quantity of half-chewed cookie.

"A simple nod will do when your mouth is full," she hurriedly said, breathing a sigh of relief when he swallowed. "So what else happened at school? Besides the spitballs."

Rob frowned as he considered what might interest her. "Freddy Dryden screamed and cried when his mother tried to leave him at the door."

"Poor boy," Liz sympathized with the youngster's fear.

"He isn't poor!" Rob took a gulp of milk. "His mom gave him a dollar to shut up. He says that if she gives him a dollar every day, he can get five dollars a week." Rob's black eyes gleamed with avarice at the thought.

"I wouldn't count on it. Sooner or later even a mother's bound to catch on," Liz said dryly.

"Do you think so?" Jaimie clearly had no such expectation of the unknown Mrs. Dryden's intelligence.

"Take my word for it."

"But—" Rob began, only to be interrupted by a loud thump as a sturdy little foot landed a firm kick in the middle of the screen door.

"Jaimie, Rob!" a small male voice demanded. "Hurry up, I'm waiting!"

"With all the patience of a whistling teakettle," Liz muttered.

"Gotta go, Mom." Rob gulped down the rest of his milk while Jaimie began stuffing cookies into his pockets.

"For later," he told her.

Liz merely nodded, having learned long ago that absolutely nothing spoiled their appetites for dinner. "And tell Ryan that if he doesn't stop kicking my screen door, I'm going to..." Her voice trailed off as the twins scooted out the door, letting it bang behind them.

"So much for the first grade." Liz wiped the cookie crumbs off the table, frowning slightly as she remembered last year and the first morning of kindergarten. When the twins had arrived home, they'd stuck to her like glue for the rest of the day. But this year, at the advanced age of six, they could barely manage to sit still long enough to relate any information. In fact, if it hadn't been for the cookies, she doubted very much they'd have stayed as long as they had.

They were growing up, Liz admitted with a pang. Growing up and away from her. Her babies weren't babies anymore, but two very distinct personalities with minds and ideas of their own. Briefly her expression softened as she remembered them as infants. All warm pudgy bodies and howling lungs. Would another child be like that? Say, a little girl? Her mind sketched an image of a small, chubby face framed by a halo of John's black hair. A little girl in ribbons and lace, happily clutching a doll.

And probably dodging spitballs. Liz smiled, remembering the twins' opinion of the female sex, then abruptly sobered as she realized where her imagination had taken her. She didn't want another child. She couldn't face another pregnancy, she reminded herself, attributing the totally unexpected yearning she had just experienced to her very unsettling day.

The thought of the day's events reminded Liz of her new book, and she decided to take advantage of the unexpected quiet to glance through it. She poured herself a cup of lukewarm coffee, took the book out of its paper bag, and went into the living room, where she sank down on the daffodil-yellow sofa. A feeling of warm pleasure at simply sitting there filled her. This room never failed to raise her spirits. The rest of the house was furnished with functional, practical furniture in various shades of brown to help hide the ravages inflicted by two small boys. But this room with its light spring colors had been designed strictly for grownups, and careful ones at that.

Liz took a sip of the fast-cooling coffee and resolutely turned to chapter one, which was titled "Establishing Effective Communication with Your Husband." She was frowning over the author's rather muddled attempts to explain the difference between communicating displeasure with your spouse's *habits* and implying a dislike of your spouse himself, when she heard the front door open.

"Use the back door, boys," she called out.

Then she jerked to attention as John's voice yelled back, "It's me, Liz."

She slammed the volume shut and jumped up, frantically looking for a place to hide it. She definitely did not want John to see the book. It would require too many explanations, and her reasons for buying it weren't any too clear even in her own mind. A quick glance around the immaculate room was sufficient to show her there were no other convenient hiding places, so she hurriedly stuffed the book under a sofa cushion just before John appeared in the doorway.

"What's the matter?" he asked, frowning at her nervous stance in the middle of the room.

"Nothing," Liz said brightly, a furtive peek at the sofa assuring her that her secret was safe. "I'm just surprised to see you, that's all. I can't remember the last time you were home in the afternoon." Today had been a day of surprises all around, she thought wryly.

"I have to go back to the hospital. I just came home for a quick shower and a change of clothes. The diaper slipped on the baby boy I was examining, and I didn't move quickly enough." He gestured toward the damp spot on the left sleeve of his shirt.

"An occupational hazard," Liz laughed. "Lead on. I'll come up and keep you company while you change."

"With pleasure." John pulled her slight body against his side, fitting her soft curves into his harder ones. For a brief, self-indulgent moment, Liz relaxed into him. The scratchy feel of his gray trousers raised tiny prickles of awareness along the slender length of her leg, bare below her brief denim shorts. As they moved toward the stairs, the muscles of his thigh rippled, sending a wave of pleasure through her body. Liz beat down an impulse to reach out and run her fingertips over those muscles. To probe their hard contours. To . . .

"Where are the boys?" John asked, clearly not as aware of her nearness as she was of his. "Aren't they home from school yet?"

"Been and gone," Liz related. "They stayed long

enough to devour a couple dozen cookies and the better part of a quart of milk. Then they left with Ryan."

"So how was the first grade?"

"Who knows?" Liz shrugged. "Their main interest seemed to be in the fact that some of the older boys taught them the finer points of making spitballs, which the little wretches then proceeded to shoot at some poor girl."

"They'll change," John chuckled as he moved aside to allow her to enter the master bedroom first. "I used to think that girls were only good for chasing fly balls in the outfield. Now, however, I can think of all kinds of uses for them." His hand slid under her thin yellow T-shirt.

"Versatile, aren't we?" Liz skipped lightly out of his reach. She crossed the expanse of thick blue carpeting to the mahogany dresser set against the opposite wall.

"Frustrating, too." John followed her, watching as she took clean socks and shorts out of his drawer.

"There you are. The personal touch." Liz tossed them onto the king-sized bed and then sat down, liking the cool feel of the sleek satin comforter against her bare legs.

"You can touch my personals anytime," John offered with a chuckle as he began to unbutton his soiled shirt.

As if drawn by the deft movement of his fingers, Liz's hands closed over his, and she pulled them down to his side. She smiled up into his relaxed face and began to unhurriedly slip the buttons free. With slow deliberation she pulled his shirt off and planted a soft kiss on the warm skin of his hair-roughened chest.

She felt his chest wall contract as his breath caught at the unexpected caress, and she rejoiced in the tell-tale sign of his excitement. They might be in their bedroom instead of in an exotic location, and she might be wearing a limp T-shirt and old shorts instead of designer clothes, but John still wanted her. The knowledge fed her self-confidence, which had taken a battering today. She rubbed her cheek over his chest, deeply breathing in the clean, masculine scent of his skin. It permeated her senses, heightening her reaction to his physical presence.

"Liz?" His voice sounded husky.

"Mmm?" she murmured as she ran the tip of her tongue down the narrowing arrow of crisp, black hair.

John's body jerked involuntarily, and Liz gave him a provocative look from under half-closed eyelids. Her hand strayed lower, rubbing lightly over the fabric of his trousers, which was stretched tightly over the re-ward of her seductive efforts. She knelt on the edge of their bed and, sliding an enticing finger just inside his leather belt, tugged him toward her. She thought-fully eyed him as if trying to decide which delights to sample first; then her lips began to gently tug the crisp hair that covered his broad chest.

She worked her way downward, running her tongue along his belt line, then moving still lower to slide her tingling lips over the wool-covered warmth of him. The tingling spread from her lips to her breasts, which were pressed against the hard muscles of his legs. Her breath escaped in a shaky sigh as she rubbed her breasts over his thighs. Her nipples seemed to swell with pleasure at the contact, blossoming into tight buds of desire, eager to escalate the pleasure.

Liz's eyes clouded with dreamy anticipation as she

focused her attention on the pressure building deep
within her.

"Darling!" His harsh sigh reverberated through his
body. His hands moved to her shoulders, their trembling stilled as they bit into her skin.

Liz barely noticed their intense pressure. Her entire
concentration was on the taste and texture of her husband's body. Finally she moved her hands to his belt
buckle and with unsteady fingers fumbled to open it.
At last it yielded to her inept handling, and, with a
sigh of anticipation, she slowly lowered the zipper.
Then she pulled his trousers down, and he quickly
stepped out of them, leaving him dressed in a pair of
briefs that did little to disguise the state of either his
mind or of his body.

Slowly Liz wrapped her arms around his hips, holding him a willing captive as she covered his sinewy
thighs with kisses.

She absorbed the fine tremors rippling through as
her hands slowly slid over his flat abdomen to caress
his hot, bare skin. The heat from his aroused body
seemed to flow into her seeking hands, gluing them
to his chest.

Lovingly she studied his emotion-tightened face.
His features were sharpened with the strength of his
desire; his eyes were closed; his gorgeous lips were
slightly parted, allowing his shallow, rapid breath to
escape. Still tantalizing, Liz allowed her fingers to
wander down his back, coming to rest on the elastic
waistband of his shorts.

She was breathing in short gasps, and a continuous
series of shivers chased each other over her skin. Her
breasts burned where they'd chafed against his legs,
and her lower body was growing liquid as John's

excitement began to swamp her senses.

What had begun as simply a teasing caress on her part had quickly escalated out of control, trapping her in her own game. She was no longer the detached temptress but instead an eager participant.

She began to remove his shorts, placing pulsating kisses on his stomach as she worked the briefs down. Down past his thighs, past his angular knees and rock-firm calves, down over his sock-clad feet.

"Liz!" The suppressed passion in John's voice skimmed over her nerves, further exciting her already receptive body. Suddenly his control snapped, and he grabbed her arms and drew her up along the length of his body.

"Seductive witch!" He grabbed the bottom of her T-shirt and impatiently jerked it over her head.

"My dear sir," Liz giggled, her laughter catching in her throat as, with a deft twist of his hand, he unfastened her bra and carelessly tossed it aside. "Whatever are you doing?"

"Playing show-and-tell," John growled as he held her away from him to allow his eyes to devour her. His gaze lingered on the pale, silken flesh of her small breasts, their pink tips hard with burgeoning passion. Deliberately, as if prolonging the moment, he pulled her into him, crushing her curves against his unyielding frame.

"You don't have to show me," Liz purred blissfully at the contact. "I can tell what you're up to just by looking at you."

"Can you?" His hands slipped inside her shorts to cup the soft roundness of her hips, and he pulled her farther into the heated warmth of his aroused body.

Suddenly a young voice splintered their labored breathing. "Wait for me!" Rob's pounding footsteps thundered up the stairs. "I gotta get my walkie-talkie. Wait."

"Hurry up," Jaimie's voice echoed faintly from the first floor.

"Hell!" John bit out while Liz stared blankly at the open doorway of their bedroom, her mind seething with yearning. Belatedly she realized she should have closed the door. But she hadn't expected things to go this far.

"Quick!" John dropped to the floor beside the bed and yanked her down on top of him, letting the huge mattress hide them from the view of anyone passing.

Liz let herself relax into him, snuggling closer to his bare chest. "We've got to stop meeting like this," she murmured.

"Quiet, wench." John's mouth closed over hers as Rob's feet pounded past, but Liz barely heard her son. Concealed behind the bed, she knew Rob couldn't see them, so she relaxed into John, parting her lips to allow the invasion of his searching tongue. Soon she dimly heard Rob slam the door to his room and retreat back to the first floor. Thereafter her entire being was centered on John—on the delightfully rasping feel of his tongue, on the caressing pressure of his probing fingers as they teased her breasts to fullness. She offered no objection when he eased her pliant body down onto the plush blue carpet.

Instinctively she reached for him, her body an overflowing vessel of clamoring need. The damp warmth of John's mouth closed over the distended peak of one taut breast, and Liz gasped in pleasure as sensation flowed through her body like molten lava.

"Now, John!" Liz grabbed his hard shoulders and pulled him to her.

"Anything to oblige a lady," he gasped. His unsteady hands slipped under her waistband, yanking off her shorts and panties with impatient haste.

Liz shivered in satisfaction as she felt the heavy weight of him settle on her. The softly abrasive pile of the carpet was an erotic stimulus down the bare length of her body, further exciting her already overheated senses.

"I love you, John Langdon," Liz moaned as he parted her legs, his hardness probing the soft, throbbing center of her desire.

As if her words had propelled him into action, John completed the embrace with a powerful surge.

Liz's thin cry of exquisite pleasure was swallowed up as his mouth closed over hers. For a second he held her still, pinned against the furry carpet with the force of his body. Then he slipped his hands under her hips and lifted her more fully into him, holding her feminine curves tightly against his solidly muscled length. He moved slowly, establishing an unhurried rhythm that quickly drove Liz wild. Frantically she twisted under him, but he refused to let her rush him. With incredible self-control, he continued his almost languid movements.

The pressure continued to build in Liz until she thought she would scream. His tongue lightly outlined her mouth, and she shivered convulsively as his teeth nipped the fullness of her sensitized lips. Finally, to her infinite satisfaction, his iron control snapped, and he began to move faster, until, with a final thrust of his body, he sent them both spinning into a mindless world of shimmering delight.

For an exquisite moment out of time, Liz lay in sublime happiness, letting her soaring mind take as long as it wanted to descend to mundane reality. Her arms closed around John's limp body as he lay sprawled above her, the picture of the supremely contented male. Her hands slid compulsively down his back to gently trace a path over his damp skin.

God, she loved him! If anything ever happened... A picture of Brandy Rome formed in her mind, and instinctively her arms tightened, as if she could physically hold her husband to her.

The increased pressure roused John, and he lifted his head to smile a shamelessly masculine smile down into her flushed face. "There," he chuckled. "Isn't show-and-tell fun?"

"Ah, but I'm a slow learner." Liz reached up to kiss his cheek, the slight roughness of his incipient whiskers tickling her love-swollen lips.

John nodded in mock seriousness. "What you need is lots of reinforcement. Fortunately for you, I have lots of patients."

"John Langdon!" Liz groaned at his awful pun. "You know what Thurber said about men who made puns."

"No, what?" He raised his upper body slightly, supporting his weight on his arms.

"He said that a man who will make a pun will do anything."

"Really?" John's jet-black eyes twinkled. "You mean things like this?" He arched forward, and Liz's eyes widened as she felt the resurging heat of him.

"Mmm, I don't know." She licked her lips distractedly as her body involuntarily responded to his quickening desire. "I don't think Thurber was implying things sexual. I mean," she continued disjointedly as John began to gently nibble on the tip of her breast, "at least not in his public statements." ·

"Speaking of public . . ." John sighed regretfully as a sound much like that of a herd of stampeding elephants advanced down the hall. He rolled off her and glanced up over the bed just as Rob burst through the open doorway.

"Dad," Rob demanded, "what are you doing on the floor? Have you seen Mom?"

"Don't come in. I broke a glass, and I'm not sure I got all the splinters up," John hastily improvised.

Liz grinned at his quick thinking. She stayed huddled on the floor while she tried to gauge whether or not she could fit under the bed if Rob decided not to obey.

"We just want some money to get something from the ice cream man. His truck's here. Didn't you hear his bell, Dad?"

"No, I was thinking."

Liz pressed her lips together, repressing laughter. She'd heard a lot of unusual euphemisms for sex in her day, but never *thinking*.

"The ice cream?" Rob said plaintively.

"Take what you want from my desk in the study," John told him.

"Ryan, too?" Rob pressed his advantage.

"For the whole damn neighborhood," John agreed. "Just scat."

"All right." Rob sounded positively jubilant as he left.

"Ha!" Liz got to her feet. "Bribing your son—and

you're supposed to be an authority on childhood behavior!"

"Sometimes the old methods work best. I can still remember my grandfather giving me fifty cents to go to the movies on a Saturday afternoon. As a matter of fact—"

The clock chimed four, and John broke off in annoyance. "Damn! I was supposed to be at the hospital fifteen minutes ago." He was suddenly the remote, completely professional physician.

Liz watched in dismay as he hurried toward the bathroom. Judging from his abrupt mood change, the last few minutes might never have happened. But they had. She drew comfort from the undeniable reality, and from the knowledge that he'd be home for dinner, too. Who knew what might happen? Who knew indeed! The corners of her mouth lifted in pleasure as she dwelled on the possibilities. Even in her unsettled state of mind it was impossible to doubt that John had been pleased with her. He'd found a great deal of satisfaction in their brief interlude.

Besides, she thought as she scrambled back into her clothes, the book she was reading encouraged people to make love in unorthodox places. Didn't the floor qualify as unorthodox? She grinned as she remembered just why they'd been hiding behind the bed in the first place. Probably the whole episode qualified as unorthodox. At any rate, it was definitely a step in the right direction. She'd have to see what she could do to improve upon this promising start at lifting their relationship out of whatever rut it had slipped into.

Definitely not a face that would launch a thousand ships, Liz concluded as she viewed her reflection in the bedroom mirror. "Probably not even a rowboat," she sighed. She was just plain average, with a fair complexion, medium brown eyes, a small nose that had the most annoying tilt at its tip, and a chin that was a shade too firm to be called truly feminine. Her shoulder-length brown hair gleamed like raw silk, but its ordinary style did nothing to enhance her looks. She really didn't look all that different than she had when John married her fifteen years ago. Except that she had a few more laugh lines around her eyes.

What she needed was a whole new look. Something to make John see her in a different light. To make him realize she was a gorgeous woman. Or at least an attractive one, she amended, admitting her own limitations. No haircut or new outfit was suddenly going to turn her into a raving beauty. But she had possibilities. All she had to do was develop them. The book would help some, she hoped. There was a whole chapter on developing oneself.

Liz picked up her notes from the dresser and gave them one last glance. Tonight over dinner she was going to implement chapter one of her book. She would engage John in some meaningful conversation, in a stimulating exchange of ideas. Her eyes skimmed over the list of questions she'd jotted down. One of them would surely serve to get him involved in some real communication.

She pressed her lips together firmly. She might not be brilliant, but she could certainly hold up her end of a discussion—at least as well as the witless Brandy. The thought of the predatory woman stiffened Liz's resolve to revitalize her marriage, and, after hiding her notes in her underwear drawer, she went downstairs to put the final touches on dinner.

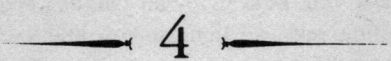

4

"MMM, YOU SMELL GOOD." John dropped a light kiss
on the nape of Liz's neck as she bent over the stove.

"John!" Her pleasure that he had actually made it
home in time for dinner was evident in her voice. She
turned and slipped her arms inside his open suit jacket
and hugged him close for a minute. "I didn't hear you
come in."

"It's no wonder," John said dryly. "The boys and
a few of their friends are out front playing some kind
of game that seems to consist of running around as if
they're demented while screaming at the top of their
lungs."

"I didn't even hear them. You get immune to the
noise after a while." She kissed his firm chin, pressed
her lips to the strong column of his neck, then raised
her head to playfully bump noses with him. "You
know that old saying about familiarity breeding con-
tempt."

"Hmm." John pulled her unresisting body closer
to him. "I like the version that says familiarity breeds."

"You would," Liz laughed, moving away as the timer on the stove went off.

As she opened the oven door and took out a steaming apple pie, John pulled his blue silk tie off and carelessly tossed it behind him in the general direction of the breakfast bar. Then he picked up a piece of stuffed celery from the relish tray on the counter.

"Nobody can make an apple pie like you can, Liz."

"Thank you, kind sir." She carefully set the pie on the cooling rack. "I'll have you know I'm full of hidden talents."

"Really?" He grinned at her. "Tell you what, I'll let you audition tonight."

"I know, during halftime." She started to make another laughing comment when she suddenly remembered her plan. Full of good intentions, she took a deep breath and launched her campaign.

"How was your day?"

"Absolutely stupendous. First, I was kidnapped by this gorgeous brunette who insisted on buying me lunch. Then"—he lowered his voice conspiratorially—"this afternoon, when I unsuspectingly went upstairs to change my clothes, this exotic woman who looked like a refugee from a *Playboy* centerfold jumped on me, wrestled me to the floor, and seduced me. Add to that a hot apple pie and the promise of a good ball game..." He sighed melodramatically. "What more could a man possibly want?" He leaned back against the counter and took a bite of the celery he was holding.

Liz watched in amusement as the smug look on his face turned to horrified disbelief.

He looked more closely at the celery's stuffing, sniffed it, and then accused, "That's peanut butter!"

"Uh-huh," Liz agreed. "It's bugs on a raft."

"What?" John stared at it, his ebony eyes narrowed in suspicion.

"Bugs on a raft. It's an old Girl Scout recipe. You fill the celery with peanut butter, then roll it in raisins."

"That's disgusting." John dropped the half-eaten stick into the trash.

"It's good for you," Liz corrected. "Lots of iron, protein, and fiber." *The boys eat it all the time, as you'd know if you were home more.* The thought flitted through Liz's mind, but she firmly squelched it. "I let the boys plan the menu, since it was the first day of school."

"Oh, no." John shuddered. "What else does this meal include besides that revolting concoction?"

"It's not too bad—shish kebab and french fries."

"How about a salad or a vegetable?"

Liz looked pityingly at him. "Don't be naive. No kid is going to pick a salad or a vegetable if given a choice. Why don't you call the boys in and ask them to wash their hands while I start the meat."

"Sure." John broke off a piece of hot piecrust as he went.

Liz frowned as she slid the shish kebab under the broiler. She hadn't gotten very far with her communication campaign. John had automatically sidestepped her leading question with a teasing rejoinder. He hadn't taken it seriously. But even while it annoyed her, she was able to draw some comfort from the fact that obviously he had enjoyed what happened today. She smiled in remembered pleasure. Lunch had been nice, but this afternoon had been nicer. Definitely an event worth repeating. She grinned suddenly as she anticipated halftime of tonight's ball game. She had thirty whole minutes, and who knew what she and John could accomplish in half an hour?

As for her abortive attempt at communication, she thought as she turned the meat, she'd have another go at that during dinner. At least he couldn't wander off while seated at the table. Balefully she eyed the slim white phone hanging on the kitchen wall. For one wild moment she actually considered disconnecting it. Then common sense asserted itself. Not only would John be furious with her, but it wouldn't really do any good. If the hospital couldn't reach him by phone, they'd simply activate his pager. She'd just have to hope that for once John's patients could manage to survive an evening without him.

Liz glanced around the table as John said grace, and her heart swelled with love. She was so lucky. She had two bright, healthy sons and a husband who, it would seem, was the envy of all her friends. Granted there were problems in her marriage, problems she had ignored for far too long. But she refused to believe they were insurmountable. She wouldn't let them be. She loved John too much to lose him. Everything would work out, she reassured herself, soothing her sudden panic. Not only had she identified the problem facing her, but she'd formulated a plan to solve it. All she had to do was to put it into effect.

Taking a deep breath, she launched into action the minute John said Amen.

"You never did tell me how your day went, darling."

"Funny, I thought I had." His black eyes gleamed with devilment.

"Besides that!" Liz nodded warningly toward the listening boys.

"Oh," he said with a shrug of his broad shoulders, "it was a typical day." He grabbed the catsup bottle from Rob before the boy could completely empty it on his french fries. "Despite what the USDA says, we do not consider catsup a vegetable in this house."

"Ah, Dad," Rob moaned, "Mom lets us."

"I am not your mother," John said mildly. "Tell me what happened at school today."

Foiled again, Liz thought as Rob began to talk. Apparently John's workday was not a subject open for discussion. Briefly she wondered if his reticence stemmed from an unwillingness to talk about Brandy, but she refused to pursue that line of thought. She knew she had no real reason to think that Brandy was any more than one of John's lost lambs, and she was determined not to further complicate an already complex situation by becoming paranoid about the woman.

"Who doesn't like you?" Liz had emerged from her musing in time to catch the last bit of Rob's complaint.

"Monsignor Brennan," Jaimie took up the tale. "You remember him, Mom," he added when she frowned. "He lives at the rectory with Father David, and he's old."

"Real old," Rob elaborated. "Even older than you."

"Absolutely ancient," Liz agreed, "but I'm sure you're wrong about his not liking you."

"No, I'm not." Rob shook his head emphatically. "He said we were rude little imps of Satan."

"Obviously a man of discerning judgment," John murmured.

Liz ignored him as she tried to unravel the story.

"Where did you meet the monsignor?"

"He came over to the school while we were waiting for the bus to pick us up," Rob said.

"Yup." Jaimie nodded. "And Mrs. Dryden was there to pick up Freddy."

"You remember Mrs. Dryden, Mom," Rob said when Liz looked blank. "She gave Freddy a dollar to shut up."

"Ah, yes." Liz nodded. "Freddy, the junior blackmailer."

"And she had Freddy's new brother with her. She showed him to us. He was gruesome, Dad." Jaimie turned to his father. "All red and wrinkled. Like your hands sometimes, Mom."

"Thanks," Liz said dryly.

"I told her she ought to see you, Dad," Jaimie continued earnestly. "That maybe you could unugly him. But I didn't make no promises. I told her you didn't do miracles."

"Oh, my God." John shook his head disbelievingly.

"You shouldn't have said that," Liz told her son.

"Why? It was the truth."

"Because you undoubtedly hurt the poor woman's feelings. All mothers think their babies are beautiful."

"Nobody could be that dumb," Rob disagreed.

"Nonetheless, you will refrain from making comments of that nature. No matter how truthful," she added when Rob looked ready to object. "And for heaven's sake, leave your father out of it."

"Why?"

"Because the AMA frowns on advertising, and I definitely don't want to get on the wrong side of them," John ended the argument.

"I guess not," Rob conceded.

"So that's why Monsignor Brennan got angry?" Liz asked.

Rob shook his head. "Oh, no. I don't know why he got mad and stomped off."

"What did you say?"

"I didn't say nothin'," Rob replied in righteous indignation. "Jaimie did."

"So what did *you* say?" Liz turned to Jaimie.

"Not much." Jaimie's ebony eyes were clearly uncertain. "The monsignor was just saying how much he liked babies, and I asked him if he had any of his own."

"Oh?" Liz replied cautiously.

"And he said the angels hadn't brought him any yet, so I said if that's where he thought babies came from, it was no wonder he didn't have any."

Liz's strangled gasp was drowned out by John's shout of laughter.

"John!" She glared at him. "This is serious."

"It's okay, Mom," Rob reassured her. "Sister Rita says it'll probably all blow over by the time we graduate."

"Sister Rita is one of the eighth-grade teachers," Jaimie explained. "She was watching the bus line."

"How comforting," Liz said hollowly.

"Sister Rita said we made her glad she decided to become a nun," Jaimie related. "Whatta ya suppose she meant by that?" he asked his father as his mother choked on her coffee.

"I wouldn't delve into it too closely if I were you," John advised.

"My God," Liz groaned, "one day of school, and you're infamous. I shudder to think what might happen tomorrow."

"But I was just trying to help." Jaimie was clearly confused.

"I know that, but . . ." Liz looked helplessly at John.

"What your mother is trying to say is that you shouldn't discuss sex with elderly priests. Or anyone else, for that matter."

"But why not?" Rob demanded. "Is sex different when you're old, Dad?"

"Sex is a private matter, not a thing to be discussed," Liz tried.

"Yes, it is," Jaimie leaped to his twin's defense. "It's discussed all the time on TV and in the newspapers and magazines and—"

"You are not to discuss sex with anyone but your mother or me." John's emphatic voice left no room for disagreement, and both boys subsided into sulky silence.

A silence Liz was quick to take advantage of. Later she'd try to figure out how to soothe the feathers the boys had inadvertently ruffled, but for now she intended to pursue her plan. If John didn't want to talk about his work, there were lots of other subjects. She hadn't spent the better part of an hour this afternoon reading *U.S. News and World Report* for nothing.

"What do you think about the situation in South America, John?"

"Not much." He deftly grabbed the shish kebab skewer Jaimie was poking at his brother.

"Did you see that fascinating article on the imminent collapse of the world monetary system?" she tried again.

He nodded. "Yes."

"Dad, will you take us to a Red Wings game?" Rob, tired of being ignored, broke in as Liz searched her mind for a new topic. A few minutes later she managed to interject another leading question.

"What do you think it would take to settle the unrest in the Middle East?"

"A miracle."

"You don't do miracles," Jaimie said. "I told Mrs. Dryden that."

He doesn't do conversations either, Liz felt like screaming in frustration, but she refused to give up. "I was reading an interesting article about Sino-Soviet relations and—"

"Sino?" Rob interrupted. "What's a Sino?"

"It means Chinese," she forced herself to answer patiently.

"Then why don't you just say Chinese? Why say Sino?"

"I don't know." Liz blinked, never having considered it before. "You just do."

John came to her rescue. "It's a combining form of Chinese derived from the Greek. It's never used alone."

"Nonetheless," Liz tried again, but before she could rephrase her question, the phone rang.

"I'll get it." John reached for it.

It was immediately apparent from John's end of the conversation that it was the hospital, and Liz felt like giving way to an old-fashioned temper tantrum.

"Sorry, Liz," John said absently as he hung up the phone. "I'll have to go in. The mother of one of my patients called the hospital to say she was bringing her toddler to the emergency room. If I hurry, I should be able to get there at the same time she does."

"But you haven't finished your dinner."

"I'll get a snack later." He picked up his tie from the counter, draped it around his collar, and began to knot it.

Knowing she was making a mistake but unable to help herself, she persisted, "Couldn't you wait and let the hospital's pediatric resident check the child first? Chances are he could take care of whatever's wrong, and if he can't, he can always call you."

"Sorry, darling." John slipped into his suit jacket. "I have to be there. The child is my patient, and her parents depend on me."

"And what about us?" Liz's voice rose shrilly despite her attempts to control it. "We'd like to be able to depend on you, too. I'm not asking you to abandon the child, for heaven's sake. You know as well as I do that the emergency room can handle anything."

"Damn it, Liz!" he shouted. "Don't make it any harder than it already is! I won't dump responsibility for my patients onto the others at the hospital. I'm going in, and that's that." He shot her a look of tight-lipped anger as he left.

"Oh, hell!" She slammed her napkin down next to her half-eaten dinner. How could she have been so stupid as to allow her frustration to push her into complaining about his leaving? She knew how he felt about being there when his patients needed him. Never before had she succumbed to the temptation to yell at him. Not even when the boys had been babies. Even then she'd waited until he'd left before sitting down and crying. So why now? she demanded of herself. Why had she suddenly exploded? The only excuse she could offer herself was that the unsettling day had thoroughly upset her equilibrium.

"Mom?" A small, hesitant voice broke into her unhappy thoughts, and she turned to find the boys staring at her, their small faces identical pictures of concern.

Abruptly she pulled herself together and gave them what she hoped was a reassuring smile. Apparently it wasn't, because their frowns deepened.

"Mom," Jaimie began, "are you and Dad going to get a divorce?"

"A divorce!" Liz gasped. For one insane moment she wondered if the boys knew something she didn't. "No." She put all the confidence she could into the word.

"But," Jaimie insisted, "you yelled at Dad, and he yelled back."

"Yeah," Rob continued, "and when Danny's mom and dad yelled and yelled, they got a divorce."

"Well, we aren't going to," Liz stated emphatically. "Look, sometimes you yell at Jaimie, don't you?"

"Only 'cause he makes me mad."

"But you still love him, don't you?" Liz insisted.

"That's different. Jaimie's just my brother. You're my mom, and moms aren't supposed to yell at dads."

Thoughtfully, Liz eyed the two earnest faces before her. Perhaps she'd done them a disservice by always hiding her anger at their father's work habits. Maybe she should have expressed it in some nondestructive manner before now.

"Moms and dads are people, too," she tried to explain, although if their skeptical expressions were anything to go by, they had their doubts. "We get mad at each other, and sometimes we yell. That doesn't mean we don't love each other. It just means we're upset."

"You're real sure you're not going to get a divorce?" Jaimie tenaciously returned to his original question.

"Yes, I'm absolutely sure. Now finish your dinner, and I'll cut the apple pie. Okay?" She smiled encouragingly at the boys, hoping they'd take the bait. To her relief, the mention of the pie did it. They began to eat, the question of their parents' unusual behavior temporarily shelved.

By the time nine o'clock rolled around, Liz was a bundle of nerves. Dinner had long since been cleaned up, and the boys were in bed, sound asleep. John had had the emergency room nurse call her to say he was tied up and hoped to be home around nine. Liz tried to believe that he hadn't phoned himself the way he usually did because he *was* tied up, not because he was still furious with her. At least he'd sent a message instead of ignoring her.

She flipped on the TV in the family room, deciding the noise would be a welcome distraction from her own disquieting thoughts. Unfortunately, she found it impossible to concentrate on the sportscaster's babble. Her mind was totally preoccupied with what she should say to John when he finally did get home. Should she take the first step and apologize? The problem with that was that she wasn't the least bit sorry for what she'd said. She'd been thinking it for years. So even if she did apologize to John, it was bound to sound insincere. She just wasn't a very good liar. She *was* sorry about the moment she'd picked to say it, though. She'd never meant to upset the boys.

She winced as she remembered their worried little faces.

No, she decided, an apology was out. Perhaps her best bet would be to simply pretend it hadn't happened, to greet John when he came home as if nothing out of the ordinary had occurred.

Maybe she should put on one of her sexy new nighties. She contemplated her reflection in the large mirror over the stereo before rejecting the idea. That would be too obvious, as if she were trying to use sex to make him forget their fight. No, better to stay dressed. She looked down at her outfit in dissatisfaction. Even though the brilliant jade color complemented her brown hair and eyes and added a glow to her smooth complexion, the style of the plain blouse and wraparound skirt was so ordinary. What had Carol said? She searched her memory. Hopelessly suburban. For once Carol was right.

Liz kicked off her sandals in disgust, wishing she owned some sophisticated clothes. Something sexy. Something to brighten up her image a little. She could always go shopping, she thought. Carol would help, and the book she'd purchased had a whole chapter on using clothes and makeup to kindle a bored husband's interest. And she'd already made a start. She smoothed her hand down over her skirt, remembering the sensuous lace and silk teddy she was wearing underneath.

The soft click of the screen door caught her attention, and she glanced up to see John.

"Hi, darling." He gave her a hesitant smile that tore at her heart. He hadn't liked their fight any more than she had.

"Hi." She smiled back. "I warmed up the TV for

you." She gestured nervously toward the bright screen.

"Thank you." John suddenly brought the hand he'd been holding behind his back around and handed her a bouquet of dandelions. "For you," he said. At her continued silence he added, "They're the only thing I could find growing in the yard."

Liz took the ragged blossoms, and her eyes filled with tears at the thought of John scouring the yard for them.

"Friends?" he asked.

Liz looked up into his anxious eyes. "Best friends." She gave him a tremulous smile. "Why don't you sit down while I put these in water."

Five minutes later, the yellow blossoms were ensconced in the place of honor in the middle of the kitchen table. Liz poured John a glass of whiskey, added some ice, and then returned to the family room. She found her husband stretched out in the brown leather recliner in front of the TV set, his eyes closed.

A feeling of almost physical pain touched her as she studied his pale features. His skin was stretched taut over his cheekbones, and tiredness had deepened the lines in his face. He looked totally exhausted, and she was shaken by an irrational hatred for the hospital and his patients, who were demanding more of him than a human being could be expected to deliver. He had to slow down. He was going to kill himself. Somehow she had to convince him of that.

She set his drink down on the end table beside the recliner, slipped off his shoes, undid his tie, and unfastened the top two buttons on his shirt. Leaning over, she began to massage his tense shoulders.

"Better?" she whispered as her fingers firmly kneaded his knotted muscles. The heat from his body seemed to flow into her fingertips, sensitizing her skin and arousing all sorts of elusive longings.

"Mmm." The corners of his mouth curled upward in a smile of pure sensual enjoyment. "Just being in the same room with you makes it better."

"Fie, and aren't you the flatterer, sir." Liz grinned at him. "You wouldn't be trying to turn my head, would you?" She could feel his body begin to relax beneath her soothing hands.

"No. Actually I'm trying to lift your skirt."

"John Langdon!"

"Well, you did ask. If you don't want to know, you shouldn't ask." He suddenly reached up and, catching her off balance, tumbled her into his lap.

"John!" Liz squeaked as she landed across his thighs.

"Phase one in my big seduction scene." He twirled the end of an imaginary mustache.

"Do tell me more," Liz giggled as she settled herself more comfortably. She snuggled her face into his neck, reveling in the slightly scratchy feel of it.

John turned up the sound on the TV's remote control unit, then picked up his drink and downed half of it in one smooth swallow.

Liz frowned as she felt his neck muscles contract. It was unlike him to gulp his drink. One cocktail usually lasted him all evening. Cautiously she tried once again to communicate.

"How'd it go at the hospital?" she probed.

She felt his body tense, and she waited for him to change the subject. To her relief, he didn't.

"Hellish!" he bit out.

Liz watched in dismay as the strong fingers of his left hand clenched.

"A fifteen-month-old toddler with a fractured skull, a broken arm, and a badly lacerated face. It'll take plastic surgery before she's normal again, but at least we were able to save her eye." He took another angry gulp of his drink.

"What happened?" Liz slipped her arms around his taut body as if trying to absorb some of his tension.

"She was riding in the front seat of the car on her mother's lap when her father stopped suddenly to avoid an accident. The child hit the dash and cut her face on the open ashtray."

"But New York State has a seat belt law!"

"Sure we do." John's voice was bitter. "But her father pointed out that he and his wife don't believe in seat belts. That whatever happens is God's will. God's will!" he spat out. "Can you believe that? I swear, I have never come so close to striking a man in my life. To hear that sanctimonious bastard pontificate about God's will as an excuse for flagrantly endangering his own child's life..."

"She'll be all right though, won't she?"

"Yes, eventually," he sighed. "But she's going to be in the hospital for a long time, and her parents will be getting a visit from the police." He shook his head resignedly. "The cops can't take any real action, but maybe they'll throw a scare into the parents."

Gently Liz pressed a comforting kiss against his cheek and silently leaned into him, giving him an opportunity to unwind before she said anything else. From the sound of things, he badly needed breathing space. But at least he'd shared what had happened when she'd asked, and that was more than he'd done in a long time. In a few minutes, when he'd had a chance to put things into perspective, she'd try to get him into a conversation that would take his mind off what had happened. But for now, John probably needed the undemanding warmth of her body more than anything else.

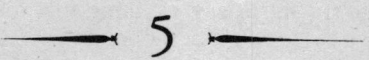

5

BY THE TIME the first quarter was almost over, the taut anger had seeped out of John's body, and Liz decided to make her move.

"John?" she murmured as she ran a fingertip along his jawline.

"Hmm?" His hand gently moved her head slightly out of his line of vision as he continued to watch the action on the screen. "Damn!" he swore. "He hit him in the hands."

Liz grimaced, knowing her presence was barely registering with John, but she refused to give up. She didn't get all that many opportunities to talk to him alone. Usually the boys were there, demanding center stage as their inalienable right. She hadn't realized until tonight just how little time she and John spent alone with each other. She thoughtfully nibbled on her lower lip. She would have to teach the boys to participate in a discussion instead of dominating it. The only question in her mind was how. A feeling of

71

helplessness at the way her problems seemed to be compounding themselves filled her, but she resolutely pushed it aside.

First things first. Before she tackled the boys' problems, she needed to rejuvenate her relationship with John. The rest would follow. What she needed now was a topic interesting enough to take his mind off the football game. Work was definitely out. The terrible tension that had filled his body was gone, and she didn't want to say anything that might bring it back.

She searched her mind for a fit subject to discuss. Something with real substance that would allow lots of room for an exchange of ideas. She'd already tried South America and the Middle East with negative results. Perhaps she needed a topic a little closer to home. Something like that article on investments she'd read in the financial section of tonight's paper.

"John, what kind of investments do you think we ought to consider?"

"What?"

Liz leaned back against his supporting arm so she could see his face and repeated, "What kind of investments do you think we ought to consider?"

"That's what I thought you said. Will you look at that!" he groaned. "They've sacked the quarterback again."

"I don't care," Liz said honestly.

"You should. I've got two dollars riding on the outcome of this game."

"Speaking of money," she interjected, valiantly refusing to give up, "what about our investments?"

"They're boring," he dismissed them, "but if you're interested, why not call our accountant and ask him to explain them to you? Block him! Oh, hell, there goes the quarterback again." He snorted in disgust.

Liz silently shared his response, but she was disgusted for a different reason. She was getting nowhere. Right now John just wasn't interested in communicating, except possibly about football. She briefly considered that topic before discarding it. She didn't know enough about the sport to carry on a rational conversation. As far as she could tell, football was an odd form of organized mayhem. Which left her with only one alternative form of communication: nonverbal.

Liz peeked at John's absorbed expression from under half-closed eyelids. Could she distract him from the game long enough to seduce him? Her body seemed to warm as she remembered that afternoon. Thoughtfully she moistened her lips and tried to decide where to begin her attack. She would have to subtly infiltrate his senses, then pounce before he realized what was happening.

She placed a series of fleeting kisses along his collarbone through the soft cotton of his white shirt.

"Can you believe that?" John didn't seem to notice her efforts. "Third and sixteen, and he calls a draw play up the middle!"

"Draw up the middle," she murmured, idly opening the two shirt buttons nearest his belt and slipping an exploring hand inside. "What should I draw?" She allowed her fingers to move over his skin in ever widening circles, smiling as the muscles of his flat stomach contracted.

"Liz, pay attention."

"I am." She gave him a look of wide-eyed innocence. "You said to draw up your middle." Her fingers slipped upward, unbuttoning as she went. "I need more room. I think I'll do a mural. A very modern mural." She gave him a provocative look.

"Liz!"

"Don't distract me." She slid her fingers into his chest hair and gently tugged. "I'm creating. Lean back, relax, and watch your game."

"How can I relax when you're—" He gasped as she gently caught one of his flat masculine nipples between her teeth and lightly circled the hard nub with the tip of her tongue. He leaned farther back into the recliner, but not to relax, she noted with approval. His body was growing tense again, but not with anger. This kind of tenseness she could cope with.

"Just watch your game while I prepare the medium. Think of yourself as a blank canvas on which I'm going to paint an impression."

"I won't be a blank canvas for long at the rate you're going." He took a deep breath as her tongue began to outline designs over his broad chest. "I'm going to be an X-rated picture in no time flat."

"I do hope so," Liz purred as she deftly unfastened his belt buckle and slipped her hands around the surging warmth of him.

"Liz Langdon, I'm afraid I'm too tired to go up to bed with you."

"Wait until you're asked," she countered. "I'm simply amusing myself."

"Trifling with my affections, are you?"

"No, with your body." She lowered her head and began to drop nipping kisses over his abdomen while her hands continued to move beguilingly over his manhood. Her eyes slid shut, the better to concentrate on what she was doing.

"Liz," he groaned, reaching down to pull her toward him. His firm, sexy lips hovered a fraction of an inch from her softly parted mouth. "You are the quintessence of seductive femininity."

"Thank you, I think," Liz muttered distractedly, her mind caught in the sensual spell she was spinning for John.

His mouth closed over hers, and his tongue plunged inside in a burst of masculine domination.

Liz moaned deep in her throat. She felt the soft contours of her body flowing bonelessly into the hard planes of his. His searching tongue was leaving a sparkling trail of excitement as it hinted of greater delights to come.

A tremor shook her as his hand slipped under her skirt, and she felt the pressure of his knuckles gently rubbing over the velvety skin of her inner thighs. She moved restlessly, opening her legs in a blatant bid for more. Slowly, much too slowly for Liz's screaming nerves, he worked his way upward toward the heated center of her desire. Liz tensed as his hand hovered teasingly, willing him to advance.

"John!" She pressed frenzied kisses against his neck.

"Liz!" His loving teasing barely registered. Her whole being was concentrated on his tantalizing fingers.

She gasped, and her abdomen involuntarily contracted as his fingertips lightly stroked the soft silk at the apex of her thighs. The warmth in her loins intensified as his caress continued. She strained against his hand, seeking closer contact, but John refused to oblige her. His fingers remained elusive and incredibly arousing.

Liz twisted on his lap, taking comfort from the

hard shape of him, which burned against her hips. Seeking to break his rigid control, she reached down to caress his maleness, but with a soft chuckle he intercepted her hands and gently held them behind her in one of his.

"Patience, my love," he murmured. His caressing fingers moved to untie the front knot of Liz's wraparound skirt, and with a firm tug he freed it and tossed it to the floor.

"Nice, very nice." The slight unsteadiness of his hand on her waist told Liz he wasn't as in control of the situation as he would have her believe.

He began to softly stroke her silk-covered skin until her lower body was a flowing mass of seething desire. Apparently satisfied with the taut muscles of her stomach, John's hand moved upward to unbutton her blouse, baring her slender body to his appreciative gaze.

"Gorgeous." He eyed the taut flesh of her breasts, their tips frozen to pebble hardness as they strained against the ivory silk. John stared deep into her brown eyes while the palm of his hand lightly brushed her straining breasts.

Liz shuddered, and her heart began to race. She tried to press herself against his hand, but he refused to indulge her. She gave a sob of frustration and took a deep breath to try to stabilize her erratic breathing. However, her action filled her lungs with the spicy scent of his after shave, and the aroma further heightened her escalating emotions to a fever pitch of excitement.

"Come, my lovely." His mouth tilted in an erotic smile as he pulled her unresisting body closer to his. His tongue danced over her sparsely covered breasts, sending tiny darts of sensation tearing along her nerve endings.

"This really is the sexiest thing I've ever seen." He pushed the damp silk teddy down to reveal one throbbing breast.

Score one for the book. The thought floated through Liz's mind a second before his warm mouth closed over her nipple and a flood of desire engulfed her body.

"I have one question," he murmured as he began to nuzzle her other breast.

"What?" Liz mumbled.

"How do I get this thing off?"

"Off?" Liz parroted on a tremulous sigh.

"So I can have my wicked way with you, preferably immediately." He dropped gentle kisses over her flushed face.

"Oh, off," Liz muttered. "It has hooks at the bottom." She jerked convulsively as his fingers quickly found the fastenings and made short work of them.

"Now, my darling, you are about to meet your fate."

"And about time, too." Liz tried to control the stream of desire shimmering through her body. "Do you want to go upstairs?"

"No." John's husky voice stroked her raging desire. "I don't think I can last that long, and the boys are safely asleep."

With an impatient movement he pulled the silken garment up to her waist. "I have a much better idea." He slipped his hands under her slim hips and lifted her up, holding her suspended above him.

Trying to force his hand, Liz rubbed the tips of her

breasts against the wiry hair on his chest. She watched in pleasure as his eyes briefly closed in the wake of the feeling she was creating.

"Ah, sweet temptress, I surrender," he groaned. His hands gently guided her downward until his pulsating desire filled her.

For a moment Liz was still. It was enough to be at one with him. She stared intently into his cherished face, watching it tighten with the intensity of his feeling.

Slowly he leaned forward to drop a soft kiss on her parted lips, then he surged upward, holding her body captive.

"John!" His name came out on a long, ecstatic sigh. She flung her head back and arched her body, trying to absorb him into her very soul.

He put his arms around her back to hold her secure. "So lovely," he murmured as his mouth closed over the roseate tip of one aching breast.

Trapped between his mouth and his arms, Liz felt him begin to move. The rhythm he established reverberated through her body, blocking out all sound, all thought. There was nothing in the world but John, his demanding mouth on her breast, his strong supporting arms around her back, his manhood stroking deep within her.

Liz's eyes slid shut, and she let his passion carry her where it would. The tension grew ever tighter until finally it snapped, hurling her into a world of unadulterated pleasure. Vaguely, in the distance, she could hear her sobs inexorably mixed with John's harsh breathing.

Liz fought her way free of the lingering haze of sensual fulfillment to find herself huddled against the damp skin of his chest, his hands gently stroking her quivering back. She made no attempt to move, content to stay where she was, secure in the loving warmth of John's embrace.

"Seven to nothing!" His outraged tones shattered her euphoric mood. "They scored!"

"They aren't the only ones who scored," Liz giggled happily. She swiftly kissed his cheek, then climbed off his lap, looking around for her hastily discarded clothes.

"There is that." His hand curved possessively over her hip as she bent over to pick up her skirt. "That really is the most fetching undergarment."

"It's a teddy." A totally unexpected feeling of shyness washed over her, and she clutched her clothes in front of her. She felt as if her plans, along with her body, had suddenly been laid bare for him to see.

"It's a vast improvement over your usual underwear." He refastened his belt. "Somehow it seems more like the real you."

Liz looked uncertainly at him, puzzled by his words but too unsure of herself to ask what he meant. Instead she nodded and scampered upstairs to take a shower, leaving him to his ball game. Today had been emotionally exhausting, and suddenly she wanted to fall into bed and let sleep carry her into blessed oblivion. Tomorrow would be soon enough to make more plans.

"No, I'll pick them up sometime this morning. Thank you, I'd appreciate that." Liz hung up the kitchen phone and gazed thoughtfully at the cheerful yellow wall in front of her.

There. It was done. Mrs. Wyvern had agreed to spend the weekend with the boys, and the travel agency had just assured her she had the plane seat next to John's for the trip to Washington on Thursday. Now came the hard part. Breaking the news to the boys. She winced at the thought of her offsprings' displeasure. They weren't going to be any too happy with this unexpected turn of events. They were so accustomed to being at the center of her universe, having her at their beck and call; they would view her going to Washington as an act of desertion.

At least John would be happy, she bolstered her sagging resolve. He'd be ecstatic that she'd elected to go with him to hear him give his speech.

The trip would also give her a wonderful opportunity to further her campaign to revitalize her marriage. All she needed now was to spend a few uninterrupted hours with her book to formulate a definite plan of action. So far the book's suggestions were proving invaluable. Her heartbeat accelerated at the memory of John's response to her new lingerie, and her face took on a dreamy expression as she tried to imagine his reaction to some of the more outrageous nighties she'd bought.

"Morning, darling." John absently kissed the air in the general vicinity of her left cheek and, sitting down at the table, looked around for the *Democrat and Chronicle*.

Liz, well aware of John's habit of burying himself in his newspaper first thing in the morning, leaped in to tell him her news before the boys came down.

"John, about this trip to Washington."

"I have to go, Liz," he said, anticipating her reaction, "but I'll make it up to you. Perhaps we can do something together later in the month."

"Sure." The bitterness she harbored toward his job

erupted before she could stop it. "In your copious free time, no doubt." The second the words escaped she wished them unsaid. John's fine-featured face took on the familiar closed expression it wore when she sniped at him about his work load.

Taking a deep breath, she tried to retrieve the situation. "Sorry, that was just a conditioned reflex. Actually, I wasn't going to complain about your trip. As a matter of fact, I called the travel agency this morning and got myself a ticket. I'm going with you." She smiled brightly, expecting him to be pleased. To her horror, he wasn't. A fleeting expression of dismay crossed his features before his face assumed what she had come to think of as his doctor's expression— calm, impersonal, and completely unreadable.

Liz felt her stomach lurch in panic. She'd never even considered the possibility that John might not want her to go to Washington with him. All her worries had been over the boys' reaction to her leaving. Now she felt as if her entire world had tilted. Doggedly she continued, refusing to let her anxiety show.

"Mrs. Wyvern is going to stay with the boys, and I'm going to see if Chris Reed will take them to a ball game on Saturday and a movie on Sunday to give her a break," she chattered brightly.

"But, Liz..." John got up and poured himself a cup of coffee, taking what seemed to Liz's taut nerves an intolerably long time to add cream. "The convention really isn't going to be a social affair. I'll be at seminars all day long, and my evenings will be filled with meeting my colleagues and transcribing my notes from the lectures."

Transcribing notes? A horrible suspicion crossed Liz's mind. Could John be taking Brandy along to type his notes? While she knew that John wouldn't have any ulterior purpose in mind, Brandy sure would. The hussy would never allow an opportunity like that to slip by unexploited. God only knew what Brandy might try, and John, despite being one of the brightest people Liz had ever met, could be incredibly naive about women—especially the predatory type. The thought of the two of them alone in a hotel room late at night was not to be borne. She had to know.

"Um, are you taking a secretary with you?" Liz forced the words out.

"No." John leaned back against the tiled countertop and sipped his coffee. "It wouldn't be worth it. The hotel's bound to have an adequate secretarial staff."

A wave of relief flowed over her, and to hide it she turned back to her breakfast preparations and began to break eggs into a bowl.

"You'd be alone most of the time," John continued.

"I know you'll be busy. Anyway, Carol's going with Gary. She and I can amuse ourselves."

"Great," he bit out. "That's exactly what I need to put my mind at rest. The thought of you trailing along in the wake of a militant feminist. You'll probably wind up chained to the fence of the capitol building to protest the demise of the ERA."

"I may not be the smartest person in the world, John Langdon," Liz snapped, "but neither am I so dumb as to get sucked into anything outrageous. At least credit me with some common sense."

John came up behind her and put his arms around her. "I'm sorry, darling." He nuzzled the soft skin at the side of her neck, and his tongue began to stroke the tiny hollow under her ear. The lemony fragrance of his after shave drifted to her nose, and unconsciously she relaxed, her body seeking his. "I'm not being very welcoming, am I? Perhaps I'm simply nervous. I'm going to give a speech, and I'm afraid of blowing it."

"You?" She turned in his arms and stared into his face, surprised at his admission. "How could you possibly be nervous? The wives in the audience won't care what you're saying as long as they can stare at your gorgeous body, and the doctors will be so fascinated by what you're saying they won't care how you say it."

"Darling Liz." He lightly brushed a kiss across her soft lips. "You're so good for my ego."

She pressed her advantage. "Then you don't mind if I come?" Maybe she ought to stay at home, since he wasn't exactly overjoyed at the thought of having her along. But if she was going to change the stagnant state of their marriage, this was too good an opportunity to miss.

"No, I don't mind. I'll have Brandy call and change the hotel reservations to a double."

And won't she love that! Liz thought gleefully, totally unashamed of the uncharitable thought.

"We'll—" she began, only to be interrupted as the boys erupted into the room. Sighing, she dropped a quick kiss on John's freshly shaven chin and turned to her sons. It would be impossible to continue their discussion now. At least she'd had longer than usual alone with him. Most often he and the boys arrived for breakfast at the same time.

"Good morning, Jaimie, Rob." She glanced over their small, identical figures as they began gulping orange juice. "Slow down," she automatically cautioned, then frowned as she caught sight of some whitish smudges on Jaimie's dark green tie.

"Jaimie, what are those spots on your tie? You couldn't possibly have gotten dirty yet."

"What odds will you give?" John chuckled.

"Oh, it's not dirt, Mom," Jaimie assured her. "The liquid soap spilled itself, and I cleaned it up." He beamed at her.

"Of course. What are ties for?" Liz muttered. Thank goodness she'd had the foresight to buy an even dozen of the things. "Take it off, Jaimie. I'll get you another one before you leave."

"Okay." He obediently removed the tie, obviously confused that anyone would object to soap.

"Dad," Rob demanded, "Ryan's mom told us that if you crack your knuckles, your fingers will fall off. Is that true?"

"No," John replied just as the phone rang.

As John reached for it, Liz grimaced at the hated instrument, knowing it would be his answering service calling. It was.

"Sorry, Liz," John said upon hanging up, "I've got to go."

"But you haven't eaten any breakfast yet," she objected.

"I'll grab something at the hospital later." He picked up his suit jacket from the back of the kitchen chair and slipped into it, then patted his pockets, looking for his keys. Predictably, he didn't have them.

"Uh, Liz, may I borrow your keys?"

"In my purse." She watched as he dug them out and then, with an absentminded smile in her general direction, left. Liz sighed. His body might as well go; his mind already had.

"Sit down, boys. I'll have your eggs ready in a minute."

"Don't want eggs," Rob answered. "I want toast and cereal."

"No eggs?" She frowned. "Since when?"

"Eggs are slimy," Jaimie explained. "Justin says so."

"Justin?" Liz tried to place the name and failed.

"Justin on the bus," Jaimie elaborated. "He's the one who taught us to make spitballs."

"He's in the third grade!" Rob said in awe-filled tones.

"He's going to be in deep trouble, is where he's going to be," Liz muttered as she got out the cereal. From the sound of things, a little of Justin went a long way.

Liz poured herself a cup of coffee and sat down with the boys as they began wolfing down their cereal. Quit stalling and tell them, she urged herself. They had to know sometime, so you might as well get it over with.

She took a deep breath and said, "Um, boys..."

Two miniature pairs of John's black eyes turned to her.

"You remember that your dad is going to a convention this weekend?"

"Yeah, he told us," Rob said.

"He promised to bring us the little bars of soap from his hotel room," Jaimie said. "You can do lots of neat things with them." His eyes took on a bright gleam, and Liz felt a moment's unease.

Liz didn't know what "lots of things" encompassed, but she was willing to bet it didn't include using them to bathe. Mentally she made a note to talk to John before he gave them the soap.

"Your dad is going to give a speech, and he particularly wants someone there to hear it."

"Not me!" Rob emphatically shook his head. "I don't understand none of that stuff."

"Me neither," Jaimie concurred.

Who does? Liz thought dispiritedly.

"You go with him, Mom," Rob suggested.

"Yeah, you go," Jaimie seconded the idea.

"You want me to go to Washington with your father?" Liz was entirely taken aback. Where was the tearful reaction she'd been expecting?

"Well . . ." Jaimie said, spinning the word out, "if Dad wants someone to hear him, and there's only you and us . . ." His voice trailed off.

"Better me than you?" Liz finished the sentence for him.

"He likes you better," Rob said, clearly attempting to soften their willingness to sacrifice her.

"He likes you the very bestest," Jaimie echoed.

"Flattery will get you nowhere, my lads. But I'm glad you don't mind. Mrs. Wyvern's promised to come and stay with you."

"She's nice," Jaimie said. "Her lap's all soft."

"Probably because she weighs close to two hundred and fifty pounds," Liz replied absently.

"Really?" Jaimie's mouth dropped open.

Too late, Liz realized her mistake. "Don't you dare mention Mrs. Wyvern's weight to her. Do you understand me?"

"But—"

"No buts and no comments about her weight. You'll hurt her feelings, and she might go on a diet, and then she wouldn't bake you any more goodies." Liz congratulated herself on reducing her argument to a level they could understand.

"We won't," Rob hastened to promise. "We love her gingerbread men."

"Good. Now you'd best get a move on. The bus comes in ten minutes, and you still have to brush your teeth."

"Aw, Mom," Rob groaned, but Liz ignored his perennial complaints about the importance of dental hygiene. She had too much on her mind, all of it disquieting.

Nobody was reacting in a predictable manner. First, John, instead of being pleased to have her along on his trip, had displayed an unflattering reluctance to spend the weekend in her company. Then the boys, who should have been tearful, had been only too eager to throw her into the breach.

Not that she'd wanted them to be upset, she assured herself, but a mild expression of regret would have been nice. She'd even have settled for a perfunctory "We'll miss you." But it appeared they wouldn't. She was nowhere near as indispensable as she'd thought — to either John or the boys.

She refused to give in to the panic nibbling at the edge of her mind. The situation was hardly hopeless. As a matter of fact, the boys' reaction was a good thing, she consoled herself. Their lack of concern over her leaving would make it all the easier for her to concentrate on her campaign to renew her marriage. She could hardly give her full attention to it if she was preoccupied with her guilty feelings about leaving the boys.

Liz had just seen the twins onto the bus and was

about to relax with a hot cup of coffee and her book when the phone rang. Surely it wasn't the hospital again. She grabbed the offending instrument and barked out a clipped "Hello!"

"What's the matter, Liz?" Carol asked. "You sound as mad as hell."

"Sorry about that," Liz apologized. "I thought it was the hospital again. Poor John had to leave before he even had any breakfast."

"Or anything else, from the sound of your frustration," Carol gently ribbed.

Liz refused to dignify the crack with a response, and Carol continued, "I just called to see how your new lingerie went over."

"Fine," Liz understated. "Actually, I was going to call you today." She paused as she tried to figure out how to word her request without giving away her motivation. Carol was a good friend, but even so, Liz had no intention of discussing the intimate details of her marriage with her. Loyalty to John forbade it.

"Are you there, Liz?"

"Uh-huh. I'm going to Washington with John."

"You are?" Carol was clearly dumbfounded. "And what do the twins think of their personal slave deserting them?"

Liz winced as she remembered just how unconcerned they had been.

"And I thought," she said, ignoring the question, "that as long as I was going, I might as well update my image a little. You know, get some new clothes, some new makeup, that kind of thing. How would you like to go shopping with me tomorrow and give me the benefit of your expert advice?"

"Update your image? Liz, what's gotten into you?

First you buy new lingerie, then you actually plan on leaving the boys for a weekend, and now you're talking about updating your image."

"Why the objections? I'm doing exactly what you've been telling me to do for years."

"Sure, but I never expected you to listen to me," Carol said candidly.

"Well, I finally have. I have no intention of going to Washington, D.C., looking like some tatty little housewife. Now, are you going to help me or not?"

"On the condition that you don't tell John I did. I don't want to get the blame if he doesn't like your new look."

"It's a deal. I'll pick you up tomorrow at ten. Bye." Liz hung up the phone. She was committed. Now all she had to do was study the chapters in her book on improving her image. She smiled to herself. After tomorrow, John wouldn't recognize her.

6

"WHAT DO YOU THINK, Carol?" Liz twirled around in a billowing cloud of emerald-green silk. "The new me."

"Now that I've talked you into it, I'm not so sure I don't like the old you better," Carol said with a frown. "You look so...so"—she shrugged uncertainly—"so different."

"I do, don't I?" Liz turned back to the mirror on the dressing-room door and stared at herself with infinite satisfaction. "I've finally got an up-to-date hairstyle." She patted the short curls, the result of the beautician's skill with a permanent. "Do you realize that this is the first time I've changed my hair since I graduated from high school?"

"I liked your old style," Carol protested. "It wasn't out of date; it was a classic."

"Cars are classics. Women are fashionable. And no one can say this hairstyle isn't fashionable."

"There is that," Carol allowed, "but I still think

you should have opted for something a little more you."

"As in staid suburban matron?" Liz scoffed. "Not on your life. I'm emerging from my chrysalis."

"Well, you certainly look like a butterfly with all that colorful makeup on. I've never seen you wear anything but a little lipstick."

"Gorgeous, isn't it?" Liz leaned closer to the mirror to examine the delicate blusher on her high cheekbones and the masterful application of eye shadow, which seemed to enlarge her soft, anxious brown eyes. "The cosmetician at the beauty shop did a masterful job. I just hope I can duplicate it."

"You'll get the hang of it," Carol said, dismissing Liz's worries. "But what about that dress? Now, I could wear it, but you . . ." She shook her head.

"I like it." Liz swung around once again for the sheer pleasure of listening to the silk rustle.

"I like it, too, but are you sure you've got the panache to carry it off? I doubt even your nighties have necklines that revealing."

"It is a bit daring, isn't it?" Liz studied her reflection in the mirror. The bodice was cut low, so low it barely covered the tips of her small, firm breasts. However, the wide ruffle outlining the décolletage helped to partially disguise that condition. For a second a wave of uncertainty shook her. The dress was so different from her normal evening wear as to be in another class altogether. But she ruthlessly stifled her doubts. She was adequately covered. There was nothing indecent about the dress. It was merely suggestive. And the book had been very emphatic: If she wanted her husband to see her as a sexy, desirable woman, then she was going to have to dress the part.

The book had been right so far, she reminded herself. John had loved her sensuous new undies. There was no reason to think he'd like this any less.

Liz slipped out of the emerald silk and carefully hung it on a padded hanger. "There, that should give me plenty to wear at the convention."

"Are you sure there isn't something we've missed?" Carol asked. "Like maybe a couple of fans and some pasties to go with this new image you seem hell-bent on cultivating?"

For a brief moment Liz's eyes gleamed as she tried to imagine John's reaction to a fan dance, but common sense quickly intruded. She'd never have the nerve to carry it off, and he'd probably only laugh.

"Save the fans till later." Liz finished dressing and checked her appearance in the mirror. "All I need now is some perfume."

"Not Lily of the Valley, I presume."

"You presume right. I want something incredibly alluring to go with my new clothes."

"I don't suppose you could make do with your old stuff until after Washington, could you?" Carol asked without much real hope. "I'm dying of thirst."

Liz stubbornly shook her head. The book had been very specific about the fact that men were conditioned by society to respond with sexual interest to the heavier musky perfumes. "All I have at home are light floral scents, and this dress is definitely not a light anything."

"I'll say," Carol agreed. "It's more like Essence of Seduction. Come on, then." She grabbed half the stack of clothes Liz had selected. "Let's get these paid for. The sooner we get your new perfume, the sooner I can get something to drink."

But choosing a new fragrance didn't turn out to be quite as easy a task as Liz had assumed. For one thing, the choices seemed endless. Complicating the matter was the fact that Liz simply didn't like any of them. After years of wearing light, flowery scents, the heavier fragrances suggested by her book seemed overpowering.

The salesclerk, after waiting for Liz to sniff her way through a few of the samples set out on the counter, retreated, leaving her on her own. Liz gamely continued sniffing, although she was fast reaching the point where they all smelled the same.

"Try this one." Carol handed her an atomizer.

Liz obligingly tried it. "It smells like a garden party on a sunny summer day. What I want is something that conveys sultry nights. Very sultry nights."

"Liz"—Carol frowned uncertainly at her friend—"is something wrong?"

"What could be wrong?" Liz parried the question. Not even to a friend of Carol's long standing could she admit her fears about John's susceptibility to the luscious Brandy—or someone similar.

"Come on! Credit me with some common sense. I've known you for how long? Thirty years? And basically you've always acted one way. Now, in the space of a few days, you've altered your behavior totally. What gives?"

"Maybe I'm having a mid-life crisis." Liz continued sniffing the perfumes.

"Don't be silly. It's men who have mid-life crises, and I know John isn't up to anything. I'd have heard about it by now."

"The CIA has nothing on you," Liz agreed, almost sighing in relief at Carol's words. She knew in her heart that nothing was going on, but it was nice to have Carol confirm it.

Carol refused to give up. "Did the Polianski affair upset you? I'll admit I was kind of shocked, but there's no reason to go overboard."

"What about the Polianskis?"

"Haven't you heard?" Carol asked in surprise. "You really should get out more."

"I will. So what happened?"

"It seemed Don joined this group to learn how to raise his consciousness, and he fell for the teacher. He left Betty and the kids and moved in with the woman."

"It sounds as if she raised more than his consciousness," Liz said tartly.

"Naughty, naughty," Carol chortled, then groaned as Liz reached for yet another bottle of perfume. "Liz, have a heart! I'm parched."

"Okay." Liz gave in. She didn't like any of them, so what did it matter which one she bought? The point was that John should like them. She picked up two that had been mentioned in the book as exceptionally seductive, caught the attention of the salesclerk at the end of the counter, and made her purchase.

Finally turning back to her thirsty friend, Liz offered, "Just to show my appreciation for all your help, I'll buy the coffee."

"Ha! You didn't listen to a single thing I said. God only knows what John is going to say when he sees that green dress. Just be sure to tell him I tried to talk you out of it."

"Don't worry. He'll love it. He's a man, isn't he?"

* * *

By the time Liz had put the boys to bed that evening, she was no longer so certain that John would like her new image. When he'd called at three to tell her not to hold dinner for him, that he'd get home when he could, she'd been pleased. She'd wanted a chance to surprise him without the boys' demanding presence. If her book was even partly correct, his reaction would make the twins' company superfluous. However, the first tiny pinprick in her bubble of expectancy had been pierced when Rob and Jaimie arrived home from school. They had taken one look at her and proceeded to inform her that her perfume smelled like the toilet bowl cleaner Ryan's mom used, and that she ought to comb her hair.

Although her confidence had been undermined, by dinnertime she'd managed to rationalize her uncertainties away, telling herself that children tended to respond negatively to any change. In a few days they'd probably be just as attached to her new image as they had been to her old.

John would love her new look, though, she told herself for at least the tenth time. She nervously studied her reflection in the mirror over the stereo in the family room. Her freshly applied makeup was perfect; her hair was the epitome of fashionability; and she had daubed one of the new perfumes on all her pulse points as recommended in the book. Even her dress was new. She patted the soft fabric in satisfaction. The brilliant lemon yellow complemented her dark coloring, and the deeply scooped neckline, which exposed the soft swell of her breasts, enhanced the sexy image she was trying to create.

Liz heard the sound of the garage door opening, and she hurried into the kitchen to meet John. A feeling of tenderness engulfed her as he walked into the brightly lit room. His broad, masculine shoulders drooped wearily, and his skin had almost a grayish tinge to it. He looked exhausted. He probably hadn't stopped for breath since he left that morning.

"Hi, darling," Liz greeted him. "Did you get a chance to eat any dinner?"

"No," John said wearily, rubbing the back of his neck. "I'm not hungry."

"What happened?"

"The usual." He tossed his jacket over the back of a kitchen chair.

Remembering her campaign, Liz refused to accept his noncommittal answer. He'd opened up Monday night; perhaps he would again.

"'Nothing' doesn't keep you out until almost ten," Liz pointed out as she poured him a cup of coffee.

"Nothing important," John clarified before he sank down at the kitchen table as if his legs could no longer hold him. "I had a preemie with respiratory problems, and I wanted to stay close until he came through safely. I used the evening to get my paperwork out of the way before we leave tomorrow."

Had Brandy been there to help him? Liz's hand clenched convulsively at the thought, but she refused to ask the question. If she started harping about the sexy Brandy, John might begin to take even more notice of his intern. Fortunately for her self-control, John's next words removed the doubt from her mind.

"I was almost through when I pushed the wrong button on the dictaphone and erased the whole damn thing."

Liz felt her tense body relax. So Brandy hadn't been there.

"Then, just as I was getting ready to leave, Mrs. Fazzino had a breech delivery."

"She and the baby okay?"

"Uh-huh." John took a sip of the hot coffee. "The baby took a bit of resuscitating, but there was no serious danger. By tomorrow she'll be—" He paused and focused on Liz as if seeing her for the first time.

Liz watched as his weary but striking face creased in a frown and a disbelieving look settled in his dark eyes.

"What the hell did you do to yourself?" he bit out.

Liz backed up a step at the vehemence in his voice. "Um, well . . . I . . ." She took a deep breath. What on earth was the matter with him? He was supposed to be intrigued, not infuriated.

John got up from the chair and made a deliberate circle around Liz, minutely studying her appearance.

She shifted restlessly under his intense scrutiny. This wasn't going at all the way she'd expected. He was supposed to admire her, and then she would seduce him. It had worked with the silk teddy, she remembered. He'd reacted exactly the way the book had said he would.

So what had gone wrong this time? Not only was he not intrigued, but he didn't seem to be the least bit amorous. Regretfully, Liz stifled a sigh and shelved her plans for the evening. Attempting to seduce a tired husband didn't faze her; John always seemed to have hidden stores of energy to draw on. But a tired, furious husband was another matter entirely. Sex and anger was not a combination she cared to experiment with.

"What did you do to your hair?" John lightly tugged the end of one tight curl, frowning when the lock sprang back to its former shape the second he released it. "Why does it stay all scrunched up like that?" he demanded.

"Because I got a permanent." Liz kept her voice even with an effort. Scrunched indeed! He made her trendy hairstyle sound like a breakfast cereal. "Don't you like it?" She patted her hair, self-conscious under his accusing eyes. "It's all the rage."

"So are a lot of things that are better left unmentioned." He paused and leaned closer to study her face. "What the hell is all that goop around your eyes?"

"Makeup," Liz managed from between gritted teeth, feeling her control begin to slip. "Everyone wears it."

"You never did before," he accused her. "You always looked real instead of like some painted mannequin." He sniffed, stepped closer, then sniffed again. "What's that smell?"

"That smell"—Liz glared at him—"happens to be my new perfume."

"You smell like a bawdy house."

"Bawdy house!" she gasped. "Why you sanctimonious nerd! How dare you come home and criticize everything about me!"

"It was easy," John purred. "All I had to do was to look at the way you've gotten yourself up, and the adjectives leaped to mind."

"Ohhh!" Liz scowled furiously at him. How could he? "What makes you such an authority?"

"I'm not," he shot back, "but I know what I like, and that"—he gestured distastefully toward her head—"I do *not* like."

"You unfeeling—" Liz's fury erupted into tears, and rather than let him know just how upset she was, she turned and fled upstairs to their bedroom.

The invitingly turned back sheets on their bed

mocked her as she entered the quiet room. Liz sniffed self-pityingly as she crossed the room to the bath. So much for her grandiose schemes. She flicked on the switch and squinted as brilliant light flooded the area.

Did she really look like . . . What had he called her? A painted mannequin. She studied her reflection in the huge mirror above the twin sinks. Anxiously she leaned closer. She wasn't used to applying eye shadow, so maybe she had been overly generous with it. But surely she didn't look *painted*. She sniffed again, and the musky scent of her new perfume assaulted her nostrils.

At least she could give up on that fragrance, she decided. It most definitely had not been a success. Bawdy house indeed! Her sense of humor began to surface, and she giggled, then frowned as another aspect of his accusation occurred to her.

How would John know what a house of ill repute smelled like? She dismissed the question the moment it crossed her mind. His insult had doubtless been but a figure of speech. She could just imagine what he'd say if she asked him, though!

"Face it, revamping your image along more sophisticated lines was a total bust," she told her reflection. Instead of being captivated, John had been infuriated. But still, she reminded herself, not all the suggestions from the book had failed. The seductive lingerie had come off well. *And* come off fast! She smiled in remembrance. All in all she was batting five hundred, and that certainly wasn't bad.

She opened the translucent glass door to the pale blue shower stall and flipped the water on. John's cracks still rankled, but she decided to accept defeat philosophically. Stripping off her clothes, she stepped under the warm jet of water, letting it wash away the makeup and heavy perfume. The hairstyle he was stuck with, she thought with an inward flash of satisfaction. She liked it, even if he didn't, and he shouldn't expect to have his own way entirely.

On that comforting thought Liz switched off the taps and began to dry herself. She slipped into the nightie she'd chosen earlier in the evening when she'd planned to seduce John. It was a masterpiece of lace, tucks, and ribbons that covered her from neck to knee. It was also almost completely transparent, and Liz grimaced as she studied her curves. Sexy lingerie was nice, but it did tend to expose one's shortcomings. Her small breasts and slender body were outlined in stark clarity instead of being hidden behind the comforting folds of her usual cotton pajamas.

If only she were more voluptuous. She frowned. No, she was fine the way she was. Her only problem was that she has been brainwashed by Hollywood into thinking a woman had to wear a 42D to be sexy.

Nervously she stared at the closed bathroom door. She really should go out and face John. As tired as he undoubtedly was, it wasn't fair to keep him waiting for his shower, despite his nasty remarks. Her temper rose at the memory, then quickly subsided. She didn't want to prolong their fight, but neither was she going to apologize.

Her face set in stubborn lines. She'd done nothing to apologize for. Well, she *had* called him a nerd, but she regretted that only because it had destroyed the sophisticated aura she'd been trying to project. What she should have done was laugh and make a joke of his imperious behavior, she acknowledged with the wisdom of hindsight. But the problem was that she really wasn't sophisticated. She was a plain garden-variety housewife, and when she lost her temper, she did things like call her husband a nerd instead of annihilating him with a few well-chosen words.

Gathering up her courage, she pushed open the door and walked into the bedroom. To her dismay, it was empty; there was no sign of John. She gulped, undecided about what to do. Surely he hadn't been mad enough to sleep in the guest room. Perhaps he simply hadn't come upstairs yet. Knowing she had to find out where he was, she opened the door and peeked out.

The hall was dark, the only illumination coming from the diffused glow of the night-light at the top of the stairs. Quietly she began to creep down the hall, pausing when she reached the boys' bath. The sound of the shower running told her where John was, but not where he intended to spend the night. She chewed her lower lip. It all depended on how mad he was.

As she considered the situation, her gaze was drawn to the door of their small guest room. The thing to do, she decided, was to reduce his options. Making up her mind, she scrambled into the guest room, hastily stripped off the sheets and blanket, and shoved them under the bed. Grabbing the pillows, she sent them under, too. There. He'd find it very uncomfortable if he tried to spend the night in here.

She hurried back to their room and slipped beneath the sheets. The central air conditioning had a tendency to be rather cool when one was wearing nothing but a drift of beribboned lace. She flicked out the bedside lamp and turned onto her side to face the wall, trying to decide whether or not to pretend to be asleep. She still hadn't made up her mind when John arrived five minutes later. She held her breath as she felt the bed give beneath his weight.

"Liz?" he murmured. She ignored him.

"Oh, hell, woman!" John's strong arms gathered her stiff body up against his chest. "Don't sulk. I'll admit I was less than tactful."

"Quite a bit less," Liz agreed, not wanting to give in too easily. But she could already feel her self-control slipping. The hard warmth from John's chest was slowly flowing into her body, eroding her defenses. Against her will, she could feel herself relaxing, her pliant frame fitting itself to his masculine contours.

"I didn't mean to hurt your feelings, love." One of his hands angled her head more comfortably into his neck. "You just took me by surprise. It was a bit of a shock to come home to a wife who's completely changed. Especially when one of the things I always liked about you was how natural you looked."

"Oh? But I can't stay the same forever. I'm not Peter Pan."

"Hardly," John said dryly, "but you'd make a great Tinker Bell."

What did he mean by that? she wondered, but she didn't want to divert the conversation by asking.

"Tell you what," John said around a tremendous yawn, "let's compromise."

"Yes?" Liz asked cautiously.

"I won't object to your new hairstyle if you quit using too much eye makeup at home and go back to your usual perfume."

"All right," Liz agreed, only too happy to have their argument settled. She was also honest enough to admit that she hadn't really liked the new perfume, and perhaps the eye shadow had been a bit too heavy.

"Good." John gathered her closer. "I love you, Liz," his sleepy voice caressed her.

Liz willed her body to relax. Much as she would have preferred a different ending to the evening, she knew John needed his sleep. And tomorrow they'd leave for Washington. The thought cheered her immensely. Anything was possible. She smiled to herself and snuggled a little deeper into his comforting hold.

Hours later the muted buzz of the bedside phone jerked her awake. With a protesting moan, she reached for it.

"Hello." She pulled herself up onto one elbow and peered blearily at the luminous numbers on the digital clock radio. Twelve forty-five?

"Mrs. Langdon?" a crisp voice demanded.

Who'd she expect? Liz thought sourly.

"Yes, this is Mrs. Langdon."

"Is the doctor there? This is his answering service."

"Just a minute." Liz rolled over and looked at John, who was lying on his stomach with his head buried under the pillows.

"Phone, John." She poked him, watching in sympathy as he opened bloodshot eyes that took a second to focus.

"Hmm?" he groaned, holding out a hand for the offending instrument.

"Just a minute," he murmured into the mouthpiece as he picked up a pad and pencil from the nightstand. "Repeat that once more, please . . . Thank you." He depressed the receiver button to get a dial tone and pulled himself up against the headboard.

"What time is it, Liz?"

"Almost one." With drowsy interest she watched the muscles ripple in his bare chest. "What happened?"

"Mrs. Carnaby called and said she had to speak to me. She told the answering service it was an emergency." He frowned thoughtfully. "I wonder what's wrong. She only has one child, and I just saw him today for his six-month checkup. He was in perfect health."

"Yesterday." Liz rolled over.

"What?"

"You saw him yesterday. It's already tomorrow. So call the woman and find out," she advised unnecessarily, since John was already dialing the number.

Liz listened to his crisp tones, from which all traces of sleep had disappeared. Attuned to the fine nuances of his voice, Liz heard an imperceptible edge creep into it. She looked up at him curiously, blinking at the thunderous expression on his face.

"You can't expect immediate success, Mrs. Carnaby. If he still isn't eating it after two weeks, call during office hours and we'll discuss it again. Good night!" His clipped tone left no room for argument. He leaned across Liz to hang up the phone.

She smiled sleepily as his well-muscled chest filled her field of vision for a brief moment.

"What was that all about?" she asked her softly cursing husband.

"Her baby boy won't eat his cereal."

"What?" Liz blinked.

"I told her today to start him on cereal, and she called to report that he spit it all out!"

"At one o'clock in the morning?"

"It seems she works the second shift and just got home."

"Why didn't you tell her what you think of idiots who call with fake emergencies at this hour of the night?"

"Because she's terribly sensitive, and if I yelled at her now, it would be just my luck that a real emergency would come up and she'd wait until office hours to tell me about it. At times like this I wish I'd specialized in dermatology." John sighed as he turned out the lights and pulled Liz back into his embrace.

So do I, Liz thought, *all the time.*

7

"WILL YOU BE all right now?" John released her clammy hand once the plane had reached cruising altitude. The quick glance he shot at his well-worn leather briefcase was sufficient to tell Liz where his attention was centered.

"Certainly." Liz forced a smile. "It's only going up and coming down that bother me. I'll be fine until we reach Washington. I think I'll just rest my eyes for a while."

The quickly concealed relief that flashed through John's ebony eyes confirmed her initial impression.

"I guess I'll look over the notes for my speech tomorrow," John said as he eagerly reached for his briefcase.

Telling herself not to take it personally, Liz leaned her head back against the headrest of the plush beige seat. After all, if she were slated to give a speech to an audience of pediatricians, she'd want to study her notes, too. Besides, she could make good use of a quiet spell to review her campaign. It seemed as if she'd been running around in a permanent state of disorganization ever since she'd seen Brandy in John's office. She wiggled slightly, seeking a more comfortable position.

So what have you accomplished? she asked herself, trying to put the events of the past few days into perspective. With the help of her book she'd managed to identify four major areas in her marriage that needed attention: her lack of real communication with John, her preoccupation with the twins, her dowdy image, and the slight stagnation of their love life. She had identified the problem areas and made a start toward solving them, even if the results had been mixed.

Her attempts to reestablish communications with John had met with only limited success. She frowned as she tried to decide why. She had followed the book's advice and thoroughly read both a news weekly and the local paper so she could engage her husband in a meaningful exchange of ideas on topics of mutual interest. Unfortunately, the book had failed to tell her how to elicit something more than monosyllabic answers.

Nor had it included advice on how to exclude two loquacious six-year-olds from the conversation. The obvious answer, of course, was to get John alone. But there again she was right back where she had started. He was rarely home for her to get alone. However, despite her setbacks, her attempts had not all been failures. He had told her about several small incidents from his workdays. Granted it wasn't much and could hardly qualify as a real exchange of ideas, but it was a start. No matter how tenuous, it was still something, and something was better than nothing.

"Would you like a drink?" The flight attendant's question broke into Liz's mental inventory, and she opened her eyes, blinking at the sight of the gorgeous redhead giving John the full benefit of her beautiful smile.

"Black coffee, please," he muttered absently, barely looking up from his notes.

"My husband's rather preoccupied," Liz said, then promptly could have kicked herself. What on earth was the matter with her? Staking a claim to John in such a blatant manner! She was much too old to do things like that. But not too secure, the unwelcome thought intruded. Liz refused to examine her unusual reaction. All she was certain of was that she wanted it firmly established that John was her personal property.

"Nothing for me, thanks," Liz added as the woman glanced at her. "I have everything I need." Or rather I would have if I could just get my act together. She leaned back and closed her eyes again, shutting out the sight of the pretty redhead.

Now, where had she been in her list? About to consider her second problem area, she answered herself. About being a supermom at the expense of being a wife. But that had never really been a conscious decision, she defended herself. It wasn't as if she had suddenly decided to begin spending more time with the boys and less with John. It had simply evolved that way. The boys had been there, and John hadn't. So she'd done extra things with them to make up for the fact that they saw so little of their father. *And* because she'd been lonely, she admitted. It wasn't a matter of preferring the boys' company to her husband's. She'd simply settled for what she could get.

But what was she supposed to do about the boys? The book's advice on supermoms—her lip curled at the ridiculous word—was hardly applicable. She couldn't integrate John into their activities and then gradually limit the boys' participation, leaving her and her husband alone together. He wasn't there to integrate. If he had been, the whole situation would never have developed in the first place.

So what could she realistically do? She could cut down on the amount of time she spent with the boys. Already school seemed to be doing that for her to a large extent. But no matter how much she limited her activities with the boys, it wouldn't increase the amount of time she spent with John. Even when he made definite plans to do something with her, there was only a fifty-fifty chance the plans would be carried out. The telephone always seemed to ruin everything. She couldn't remember the last time they'd gone to a party and come home together.

Why, he hadn't even been with her the night the twins were born! One of his patients had needed him, and off he'd gone. If she dropped dead, he probably wouldn't even notice until he ran out of clean shirts!

At least she'd been able to change her dowdy image. The thought of her new clothes and hairstyle cheered her momentarily. Then her pleasure faded slightly as she remembered John's reaction. He had definitely *not* been too enamored of the new Liz Langdon. But maybe she shouldn't have been so surprised. The book had made a big point of the fact that men, like children, were basically conservative creatures who resisted change.

But if that was true, then why did so many men divorce their wives and take up with younger women?

The inconsistency of it made her uneasy, and she shifted restlessly. While she was hardly naive enough to take any self-help book as absolute fact, she did wish its errors in logic weren't quite so glaringly obvious. On the whole, though, despite its flaws, it was the only guide she had. And it did contain some good advice, at least on undergarments. Apparently it was all right with John if she changed her image, as long as the change didn't show in public. She grimaced at the convoluted workings of the masculine mind.

If John weren't such a wonderful person, and if she didn't love him madly, she'd forget the whole thing. But he was a wonderful person, she thought wistfully. He was also a fabulous lover. Which brought her last point to mind—getting their love life onto a plane of consistently higher excitement.

She'd made a good start on that particular problem, she reflected smugly. She ran her tongue over her lower lip as a flush stained her cheeks at the memory of their tryst in the recliner. This extended weekend away from the boys and John's practice should provide lots of opportunities for a freer expression of their love. She giggled as she remembered hiding behind their bed. The authors of child-rearing books never warned you about those kinds of parental hazards.

A shiver chased over her skin as she felt a finger lightly trace her ear. She opened her eyes and found herself looking into John's smiling face. For a mad moment she considered trying to seduce him right then and there, but reality promptly intruded. One could go only so far in adding spice to one's sex life. She turned her face into his large palm and pressed a kiss in it, then lightly teased it with the tip of her tongue.

"Finished?" she murmured.

"Lady, I haven't even started." The kiss he dropped on her softly parted lips convinced her they were discussing two entirely different matters.

"I meant with your speech." Liz nodded toward the pile of scribbled notes on his lap.

"No, I was too busy watching you. The expressions on your face were indescribable. It was like watching an actor give the full range of his emotional repertoire. What on earth were you thinking about?"

"I was plotting our weekend," she said, giving him part of the truth. "I have lots of plans."

"So do I." His firm lips curled in a sensual smile.

"You mean your speech?" Liz batted her lashes theatrically.

"What I have in mind doesn't require any words. It's strictly tactile."

"Sounds like touch-and-go to me," she punned, grinning.

"That's it exactly. How nice to know we understand each other." He grinned back, his teeth gleaming white against his dark skin.

If only we really did, Liz thought despairingly as she anxiously searched his beloved face for a clue to his real feelings.

"What's the matter, darling?" John's voice was gentle. The backs of his fingers lovingly stroked her cheek. "Are you still upset that I didn't like your tent?"

"It isn't a tent!" Liz said crisply. "It's a tunic, and tunics are considered high fashion right now."

"Not with me they aren't. I used to sleep in something like that when I went camping with the scouts. It was even the same color." He cast a disparaging glance at her khaki silk tunic.

"I'll bet it didn't cost as much," Liz shot back.

"Do you know what I paid for this?"

"They should have paid you to wear it," he sniped.

"Philistine!" Liz sniffed.

John shrugged. "I'm a man, and men like to have at least some idea of what a woman's body looks like. The only people who should wear sacks are the ultra fat and the ultra thin. Definitely not a woman with a shape as lovely as yours." His hand audaciously cupped the underside of her breast.

"John!" Liz hurriedly glanced around.

"I already looked," he confessed with a chuckle, "and your modesty is intact. The man across the aisle is asleep."

"Yes, but . . . but you still shouldn't," she finished feebly.

"Sometimes I get sick to death of doing what I'm supposed to do," he ground out.

Liz blinked uncertainly, wondering what he'd meant by that. Was he referring to their marriage? His job? Both? There was no way to tell, and she didn't want to ask him. She might not like the answer.

"Liz . . ." He picked up her hand and, turning it over, began to absently rub his thumb over her palm. "Darling Liz."

She tried to ignore the sensation radiating from his absentminded caress and concentrate on what he was saying.

"I haven't been fair to you, have I?" He gave her a lopsided grin, and Liz's stomach felt as if she'd just dipped down one loop on a roller coaster. She could feel her entire body grow taut in response to his words. What if the boys had had a point about divorce? Was this where John offered to do the honorable thing and give her her freedom? To her indescribable relief, he didn't. His mind hadn't been running along the same lines as hers, and, as a result, it took a few seconds for his words to penetrate.

"You've obviously gone to a great deal of trouble, what with that hairdo"—he viewed her curls with disfavor—"and your new clothes. And instead of supporting you, I've been unforgivably critical."

"The alternative would be to lie to me, and I think I prefer honesty. In fact, I know I prefer honesty," she added emphatically.

"It wasn't your new clothes that bothered me," John replied. "It's just that you caught me off-balance." He frowned slightly as if trying to find the words to express himself. "You see, you're the one reliable thing in my life. The one thing I can count on absolutely. You're not always in the best of moods, but you're always there. The safe center of my world. And it shook me to come home and suddenly find you changed."

A feeling of sheer relief lent brilliance to the smile she gave him. "But I'm still the same underneath."

"An idea definitely worth exploring." He smiled wolfishly.

"It's just that with the boys gone all day, I decided to shape myself up," she said, editing out her deeper reasons.

"Liz"—he paused uncertainly—"if you miss the twins, we could always have another child."

Liz reacted instinctively. "You have trouble enough finding time for the boys," she said sharply. She could have bitten her tongue when he visibly flinched.

"Oh, John." She impulsively touched his sleeve, but his movement to pick up his notes shook her free.

"As you say, I'm not superb father material," he

said distantly as he began to study his notes, effectively shutting her out.

Liz swallowed unhappily as she retreated into her seat. That wasn't what she meant! she wanted to protest. He wasn't a bad father. He wasn't! What little free time he did have he lavished on the twins. Somehow he always seemed to dredge up some time for them. Not necessarily for their mother, she thought bitterly, but always for the boys.

She saw so little of him as it was, and if there were yet another child demanding his attention... Her mind shied away from finishing the thought. She wasn't jealous of the time John spent with the twins, she assured herself. She wasn't. No decent mother could be. With an unhappy sigh, Liz got her new novel out of her purse and tried to interest herself in it. She might as well; she'd probably be spending a lot of time with it this weekend if John's present mood lasted.

Maybe she'd made a big mistake, she thought as she stared blankly down at the first page. Maybe she should have found out whether it was really feasible to regain an active role in John's life before she'd begun to separate herself from the boys. He certainly seemed to want her around, she reflected, recalling his recent words, but simply being around was hardly a stable basis for a marriage.

Trying not to think about it, Liz forced herself to concentrate on the meaningless words before her. Unbidden, her eyes strayed to John's implacable features, and her heart sank. The eagerly awaited weekend seemed doomed, and she had nothing to blame but her own hasty tongue.

Fortunately, by the time they reached the hotel, John seemed to have put his anger behind him, and he responded to her hesitant queries about the convention with his customary good humor. Liz was exceedingly grateful.

The hotel they were staying at was the most elegant place Liz had ever seen. When they were first married, a dinner out had been a big treat; a weekend away had been far beyond their slender means. Later, when money was no longer a problem, they'd had the twins, and not even a doting mother like Liz would have presumed that two active youngsters would be welcome at a place like this.

She smiled at the uniformed doorman who held open the gleaming glass doors for them. She instinctively edged a little closer to John as they crossed a vast expanse of thick red carpeting.

John glanced at her. "What's wrong?"

"This place makes me nervous," she admitted. "I keep wanting to check and see if my slip is showing."

"It isn't," John chuckled. "The only things showing are your very shapely legs."

Liz felt a comforting glow at his compliment, and she was able to approach the wide marble reception desk with something approaching her usual self-confidence.

Instead of the supercilious clerk Liz was dreading, they were greeted by a well-dressed man in his fifties who exuded warmth and who seemed genuinely glad to see them. He gave John such a broad smile as he handed them their room key that Liz began to wonder. Had her campaign been even more successful than she'd thought? Did she look so sophisticated that the hotel clerk thought she was John's mistress rather than his wife? That must be it, she told herself happily.

She was making progress. At least she hoped that was progress.

She looked at her husband, wondering if he'd noticed the admiring gaze the man gave her. Although normally very perceptive, on occasion John could be remarkably obtuse. It appeared this was to be one of those times. He met her questioning glance with a quizzically raised dark eyebrow. Liz simply shook her head and continued along behind the bellman.

The elevator shot soundlessly up to the third floor and disgorged them into a wide hallway, where the same thick red carpeting cloaked the floor. The bellman stopped in front of a pair of carved double doors, unlocked them, and stepped aside to allow Liz and John to enter.

"We hope you enjoy your stay," he said. "The champagne and roses are courtesy of the management."

Liz wandered across the thick cream-colored carpeting, staring around with disbelieving eyes as John tipped the bellman. The living room of the suite looked like a movie set, and a high-budget one at that. A highly polished credenza had one door ajar to allow a glimpse of what seemed to Liz a vast amount of liquor. Two white linen sofas faced each other across a large glass-and-brass coffee table. On it stood a silver bowl filled with dozens of deep red roses. An assortment of fragile-looking gilt-trimmed furniture was scattered about the large room.

Red roses for his true love? Liz briefly entertained the idea before reluctantly dismissing it. The bellman had specifically said the roses were a gift from the management. He'd also said something about cham-

pagne. She frowned, casting a quick glance around
the opulent surroundings. Unless it was hidden in the
credenza, the champagne was nowhere to be seen.

She assumed the door in the far wall led to the
bedroom, and, curious, she opened it. She gasped.
Not even the luxury of the outer room had prepared
her for this. Directly in front of her was a huge heart-
shaped bed set on a carpeted dais. Yards and yards
of billowing pink silk were suspended from a heart-
shaped canopy mounted on the ceiling above the bed.
She crossed the plush carpeting and climbed the three
steps to the bed, amazed that such a thing really ex-
isted. She idly wondered where they bought sheets to
fit it.

She tore her gaze away and looked around, dis-
covering the champagne nestled in an ice bucket beside a pink chaise longue.

All the suite needed to complete the picture was
Mae West. Liz felt sheer happiness bubble through
her veins as the reason for the clerk's manner suddenly
became clear. This had to be the honeymoon suite!
There was no other explanation for the sybaritic splen-
dor of it. And John had reserved it himself!

Too happy to sit still, she went through the other
doorway in the room. It was the bath, if such a bac-
chanalian room could be called something so plebian.
In stark disbelief Liz stared at the heart-shaped pink
marble sunken tub. Golden cherubs served as faucets.
The rather ordinary shower stall she ignored in favor
of admiring the twin, heart-shaped sinks in the wall-
to-wall vanity. Beside them, ivory shells held tiny
bars of pink heart-shaped soap.

Thoughtfully she swung her gaze back to the bath,

and an idea burst full blown into her mind. Add variety to your sex life by varying the location, the book had said. What could be more varied than making love in the bathtub? It was certainly big enough. They could practically hold a cocktail party in it.

Making up her mind, she flipped the taps on.

"So this is where you got to." John's indulgent voice came from the doorway, and Liz jumped.

"Oh, John, thank you!" She beamed at him. "It's absolutely . . ." She waved her arms around the room expressively.

"Decadent?" He picked up one of the small bars of soap and eyed it incredulously before dropping it back.

"Romantic is what comes to my mind." She slipped her arms into his open suit jacket and pressed her body against his. "Vulgarly romantic. I love it."

"Good." He dropped a light kiss on her upturned nose. "I couldn't afford anything like this when we were first married, and I always wanted to make it up to you."

"Make what up to me?" Liz leaned her head back and stared into his charcoal-black eyes.

"Those two nights of our honeymoon at that back-water motel that was little more than a truck stop."

"John Langdon, I don't want them made up for!" she said vehemently. "I had a wonderful honeymoon. You were the most fantastic lover a bride could have wanted. Who cared what the room looked like? We never got out of bed anyway."

"True." He laughed, then observed, "Your tub's about to run over."

Liz hurriedly turned off the cherub fixtures. "Why

don't you have a long soak while I go downstairs and find the man who's in charge of the opening session," John suggested.

"You have to go now?"

"I told the moderator I'd go over my speech with him when I arrived."

"But it's early yet," Liz pouted as she lightly ran her fingertips over his sensual lips. "And you can't go visiting when you're all hot and bothered."

"Being around you is what makes me hot and bothered."

"I know just the thing to cure that, and half an hour won't really make any difference, will it?" Liz murmured the soft words against his jaw, then took a deep breath, inhaling the scent of his after shave. "Mmm." She gave a contented purr and slid her body down his hard length. She could feel her breasts tautening and a warmth beginning to grow deep within her. "You climb into the tub, and I'll scrub your back."

"A hot soak sounds heavenly," he said, obviously weakening. "And you're right; half an hour won't really make any difference."

"Fine." Liz used his tie to pull his head down in order to place an inviting kiss on his lips. "You climb into the tub, and I'll set out your clothes." She grabbed one of the huge pink bath sheets from the heated towel rack and hurried into the bedroom.

So far, so good, she encouraged herself. She'd gotten him into the tub. Captivating him into some decadent lovemaking wasn't going to be any problem. She remembered the feel of his hard body pressed against hers. The problem was going to be avoiding drowning. She smiled happily. Ah, well, life was full of risks.

Anxious to return before John's overdeveloped sense of duty reasserted itself, Liz began to fling off her clothes, paying no heed to where they landed.

Once naked, she wrapped herself in the fluffy pink towel, tucking the loose end between her breasts. She frowned slightly as she studied her image in one of the bedroom's many mirrors.

"All you need is a rose between your teeth," she muttered.

"Liz," John called, "you promised to scrub my back."

"Coming!" She hurriedly fluffed her curls and, picking up the bottom of the towel, sped toward the bathroom.

John was stretched out in the huge tub, his dark head resting against one of the curves at the top of the heart, his eyes closed.

Liz gulped as her gaze was drawn to his lean, athletic shape, which seemed to buoy and sink with the gentle movement of the water.

She knelt down beside the bath and, picking up one of the pink soap bars, worked up a lather. Leaning forward, she cupped her hands around his neck and began to gently rub the sweet-smelling soap into his skin. His flesh felt firm and supple beneath her fingers, and she sighed with pleasure at the feel of him.

The steamy cloud rising from the water enveloped her, sensitizing her skin. Slowly her hands slipped lower, over his shoulders, and she frowned slightly. He really was tense. She looked into his face, but his eyes were still closed.

Her breath caught in her lungs as her attention was compulsively drawn to his beautiful mouth. A wave of desire shook her, but she resisted the impulse to kiss him. She reminded herself that her plan called for her to tease and tantalize him, to drive him mad with longing. Provided she didn't go mad first, Liz thought ruefully. She wasn't sure she could be detached enough to do a truly memorable job.

John's deep contented sigh filled the room, and, encouraged, she allowed her hands to drift still lower under the hot water. Her eyes slid shut, and she began to explore his chest. Gently she outlined one of his hard masculine nipples with a probing finger, gently flicking the pebble-hard tip with her fingernail.

Her lips curved upward in a dreamy smile as his body jerked convulsively under her questing fingers. Her hands continued on their downward path. Down over the arrow of his dark hair. Its crisp, abrasive quality combined with the heat from the water was wreaking havoc with her concentration. Her breasts seemed to be absorbing the damp warmth, swelling to aching fullness. Her breathing was becoming erratic, and the tightening knot of desire in her loins was screaming for relief. But still she held back, determined to prolong the moment.

Her seeking fingers slid down over his flat stomach, pausing for a moment to explore his navel. Finally she allowed herself the pleasure of drifting yet lower. Her insides lurched happily as she lightly touched the rigidity of his desire. Teasingly, she continued to play as she tried to decide her next step. But with the quickness of a pouncing tiger, John took the decision out of her hands. He reached out a wet arm and swept her into the tub's heated depths. His hand began to strip away the bath sheet, and Liz frantically twisted her body to help him.

Finally they tossed the soggy, clinging towel aside, and John pulled her to him.

"Oh, God, Liz, I want to go slowly, but I need you so much." He slipped his hands under her arms and pulled her tightly against him, crushing her to his slippery chest.

A wave of exquisite pleasure shook Liz as the sensitive tips of her breasts met his rasping hair. She whimpered in mindless satisfaction as his hands closed around the velvety skin of her buttocks and levered her buoyant body up out of the water to allow his seeking mouth to close over the hard tip of one breast.

"John!" She clutched his steam-dampened hair, holding his devouring mouth tightly against the soft, throbbing mound. She was barely aware of each separate pleasure point, so diffuse was the feeling of enchantment that filled her.

"I'm sorry, Liz," John gasped, "I can't—" His meaning became crystal clear as, with a powerful thrust, he merged their sleek, heated bodies, making them a single entity with but one thought: their mutual satisfaction.

Liz shuddered uncontrollably and grasped his shoulders as her hard-driven senses propelled her into a world of pure sensation. The rigidity of John's body thrusting into her, the rhythmic lapping of the water, the curiously hollow sound of their erratic breathing in the cavernous bathroom—such was her sole reality. At that moment she was incapable of rational thought, only of feeling. Feeling that was turning her into a writhing creature seeking glorious fulfillment. And then fulfillment was hers. Divinely. Exquisitely. Totally.

After several minutes, John's gentle lips caressed her damp forehead. "Liz?"

"Hmmm?" She blissfully snuggled her wet cheek into his chest, coughing slightly as she accidentally got a mouthful of water.

"Liz, this time I really do have to go."

"Okay," she yawned. "You go do your thing. I intend to take a long nap."

"Good idea." He picked her up and deposited her dripping body on the thick white bath mat, his firm hands steadying her when she stumbled. "It'll get you into shape for tonight."

"Lecherous man." Liz gave him an enchanting smile. "I do believe you brought me to Washington with ulterior motives. At least, I certainly hope so."

8

"THERE." LIZ ADDED a final touch of the light floral fragrance John preferred and stepped back to study her appearance.

"Very nice," she complimented herself, fiddling with a ruffle along the deeply scooped neckline of the emerald-green silk. "Very nice indeed!" She twirled around, sending the skirt swirling out in a cloud of rustling perfection. She lost her balance and staggered as one of her three-inch heels caught in the deep pile of the bedroom carpet.

Righting herself, she glanced down ruefully at the offending black leather sandals. She'd probably break her neck before the evening was out, but it would be worth it. Not only were the sandals the last word in fashion, but they made her feet look positively dainty. Satisfied she had made the most of her potential, Liz picked up her small evening purse from the dresser and turned to leave the room. The huge heart-shaped bed caught her eye, and a dart of anticipated pleasure shafted through her. "Later," she whispered.

A sharp rap on the outer door of the suite claimed her attention, and she hurried through the living room to answer it, hoping it would be John. He'd said he had to see someone and that he'd meet her in the lobby, but perhaps he'd finished earlier than he'd expected and decided to come back for her. The fact that he didn't have his key was normal enough.

To her disappointment, her caller was Carol.

"Don't look so pleased to see me," Carol said dryly. "It might go to my head."

"Sorry." Liz moved back and waved her friend inside. "I was hoping it was John."

"He's down in the lobby with Gary. We ran into him when we checked for messages. He invited us to go to dinner with—" Carol broke off in astonishment as she took in the room.

Liz quickly masked the disappointment Carol's words caused. She'd been looking forward to going out to dinner with John without his pager making a threatening third, and now he'd asked friends along. Blast! Didn't he want to spend the evening alone with her? Probably he hadn't even thought about it, she conceded ruefully. More than likely he'd simply seen his friend and automatically extended an invitation.

Determinedly, she forced a welcoming smile to her lips. What was done was done, and there was no reason to hurt Carol's feelings. But if John thought he was going to spend the evening talking shop with Gary, he was in for a surprise! She intended to keep his attention firmly centered on her, if she had to grab his tie and hold it. She hoped it wouldn't come to that. She mentally ran through the list of techniques gleaned from her book to keep a male's attention from straying.

"My God, Liz!" Carol peered into the liquor-filled credenza. "This is a hotel room? I've been to home shows that haven't been this elegant."

"If you think this is something, come and see the rest of it." Liz led the way into the bedroom.

"I don't believe it!" Carol gasped as she saw the heart-shaped bed.

"It's got a heart-shaped tub, too," Liz volunteered. "Pink marble with little gold cherubs for faucets."

"This I've got to see." Carol disappeared into the bathroom. A moment later she was back. "You didn't tell me the tub was big enough for two," Carol quipped, then hooted with gleeful laughter as a bright tide of red stained Liz's cheeks. "Well, well, will wonders never cease?" she continued teasing. "Just think, good old conventional Liz cavorting about in a decadent bathtub. Heavens, even the cherubs are leering!"

Carol frowned and glanced around the bedroom again. "Say, this monument to romantic love wouldn't happen to be the honeymoon suite, would it?"

"What took you so long?" Liz grinned. "I figured it out as soon as I saw the bed."

"Figured it out? You mean you were put in here by accident?"

"No, by John. It was a surprise."

"You lucky woman!" Carol was frankly envious. "Gary's idea of a surprise would be to forget to make reservations in the first place. Speaking of our husbands, we'd best get moving. We have to eat early because we're going to a party at nine."

"A party?" Liz trailed along behind her.

"You aren't invited," Carol said bluntly. "One of my sorority sisters has a husband who's pretty high up in diplomatic circles, and she wangled tickets to this affair for me and Gary. I could try..." Carol began hesitantly.

"No, thanks." Liz disclaimed all desire to attend, beginning to feel better. At least she'd have John to herself after dinner. Her thoughts strayed back to the huge bed. Later they would most definitely be alone.

"You have plans of your own?" Carol asked.

"Uh-huh. I've always wanted to see the Lincoln Memorial."

"It figures," Carol sniffed. "Sight-seeing! Liz, you are hopelessly suburban."

The memory of her romp in the tub that afternoon flitted through her mind, and a secret smile tugged her lips. "Not entirely," she murmured, untouched by Carol's good-natured condemnation.

Carol glanced up quizzically at Liz's enigmatic statement but seemed to lose interest when Liz didn't elaborate.

The two men were waiting in the hotel's spacious lobby. Liz's heart swelled with love as she studied the attractive figure John cut. From the top of his gleaming black hair to the tips of his polished shoes, he was the epitome of a confident, successful man.

"Hi, darling." John smiled at her, and Liz smiled back, the shared memory of their lovemaking creating a warm link between them.

"You look lovely." His eyes lingered on the firm swell of her breasts visible above the folds of the ruffle.

"You do, too, in a very masculine way." She ran a finger over the pristine whiteness of his shirt collar, unnecessarily straightening the knot of his navy silk tie, and trailed her hand down the lapel of his gray suit jacket.

John captured her hand in one of his and gave it a squeeze. "I love you," he whispered as he planted a welcoming kiss on her cheek.

Liz gave him what she hoped was a seductive smile from under half-closed eyelids, but she had her doubts when she saw his lips twitch.

"Let's go," Carol demanded impatiently. "I'm starved. Where are we going to eat?"

"I already had reservations at Le Bavarois for Liz and me, and it was easy enough to get it changed to a table for four," John answered as he took Liz's arm.

"What's this place like?" Liz asked curiously.

"French," Gary answered her, "as in expensive."

"Lead on," Carol said, grabbing his arm. "It sounds exactly like my type of restaurant."

Not mine, Liz thought worriedly. Most definitely not mine. She couldn't speak a word of French, so she'd probably wind up with a plateful of buttered snails. She shuddered at the thought, and John glanced questioningly at her.

Liz smiled reassuringly at him, refusing to voice her doubts. He had obviously planned this evening as a treat, and she wasn't about to let her insecurities ruin the evening before it had even begun. She had memorized all the advice from her book, hadn't she? she encouraged herself. What could go wrong? A whole variety of possibilities crowded into her mind, and she hastily banished them. She was going to enjoy herself, even if it killed her.

As it turned out, even the gregarious Carol was

daunted by the Old World elegance of Le Bavarois.
A thick gray carpet muffled their footsteps as they
followed the ramrod-straight back of the maître d'.
With the dignity of an archbishop the man seated them
at a table far enough away from the other diners to
allow a degree of privacy.

Liz sank down onto the red damask chair and studied the colorful spider mums arranged artfully in a
low porcelain bowl. A gleaming white linen cloth
covered the round table, which was set with what
looked like real Waterford and Wedgwood. Liz suppressed a plebian urge to turn her plate over and check
it for a hallmark.

Carol was not so inhibited. She lightly flicked the
wine glass with her fingernail, giggling when its resonant tone proclaimed its crystal purity. Liz glanced
at the maître d', blinking when he gave her a very
dignified wink. She smiled back tentatively, beginning to feel better. So what if she wasn't accustomed
to restaurants in which diners used three forks and
four spoons? The people working here were simply
people, too. Hadn't that wink proved it? The maître
d' probably had a couple of grandchildren whom he
spoiled rotten and a sweet little wife who nagged him
to take out the garbage.

It was definitely going to be a lovely evening. She
smiled happily at John and, suddenly remembering her
plans, lightly ran her finger over the back of his hand.

"I like your choice of restaurants," she told him.

He captured her hand. "Yes, I have excellent taste."

"Break it up, you two," Carol jovially commanded.
"You can do that later. We have to order now."

Sighing, Liz accepted a large leather-bound menu
from the waiter. For now she would concentrate on

dinner, but later... A quiver shot through her at the thought. Later belonged to her and John.

By the time dinner was over, Liz was in a much more relaxed frame of mind. The food had been superb, and the service, contrary to her initial fears, had been unobtrusive. She took another sip of her liqueur and smiled rather hazily at John.

What she needed was some fresh air. What with the pre-dinner daiquiri, the wine with her meal, and the cordial she was now sipping, she had long since gone far beyond her normal consumption of alcohol. Not that she was drunk, simply a bit muddled. A good brisk walk in the evening air would restore her clarity.

She gave John another smile and set down her nearly full glass. She shouldn't have ordered it in the first place. It would be horrible if she fell asleep before they could make love. She giggled at the thought.

"Liz Langdon," Carol teased, "I do believe you're tipsy."

"No, I'm not." She gave a tremendous yawn. "Just sleepy."

"At eight-fifty?" Carol asked in disbelief. "You're getting more like the boys by the moment. I can't believe you aren't champing at the bit to get back to the hotel and call them."

"I did that before I got dressed," Liz admitted.

"So how are they surviving?" Gary asked kindly.

"Just fine." Liz's voice was wry. "They informed me that the baby-sitter had made them fudge brownies with peanut butter chips after school, and then they demanded to know what I was bringing them from Washington." She gave Gary a bright smile, hoping that the hurt she felt at the boys' ready acceptance of her absence wasn't showing.

"You're to be commended on raising two such self-reliant youngsters," Gary said calmly.

"Thank you." Liz smiled gratefully at him, taking comfort from his words. It wasn't as if she wanted the boys to be heartbroken that she was gone, but it would have been nice if they'd at least said they missed her instead of simply rhapsodizing about Mrs. Wyvern's brownies.

"I don't know about you two, but we have to go," Carol announced, glancing at her thin gold dress watch.

"Do you want a lift?" John asked. "Liz and I have rented a car for the weekend."

"No, thanks," Gary declined. "We'll take a taxi."

"We're going to see the Lincoln Memorial," Liz told Gary. "The guidebook says it's a sight not to be missed."

"Guidebook!" Carol's thin eyebrows almost disappeared into her artfully arranged hair. "Don't you dare bring a guidebook along when you're out with me. Everyone will know we're from the sticks."

"Rochester is *not* the sticks," Liz objected as she rose to leave. Predictably, Carol ignored her.

Twenty minutes later she and John stood in front of Lincoln's massive monument, and Liz was doubly glad she hadn't traded this moment for a smoky party. The way the fading daylight bathed the structure in the fiery glow of sunset was something she would always remember. The almost supernatural quiet was unbroken except by the sound of their own footsteps. Liz looked up at the shadowy marble statue of Lincoln sitting in his chair, and she felt a timeless magic flow over her.

"You can almost feel his presence," John said in

a hushed voice. "As if he were watching the watch-
ers."

"I wonder what he thinks of what we've done with
his legacy."

"He's pleased, I imagine." John put an arm around
her shoulders and pulled her to his side. "We haven't
reached all his goals, but we're trying, and that's all
anyone can ask."

A raucous burst of music shattered the unnatural
calm, and Liz jumped, looking around in surprise. A
set of parents and their obviously bored teenager—
his ear glued to a blaring radio—were climbing the
broad steps.

Liz sighed as the discordant noise increased in volume, and of one accord she and John turned to walk
back to the car. They were passing a play area when
loud voices caught Liz's attention. She looked in
the direction of the sounds.

A mother was trying to persuade her young son to
leave the nearby playground and go home to bed.

"Sweet reason isn't going to get her anywhere,"
John chuckled. "She'd do better to grab him by the
scruff of the neck and drag him off."

"Yes, I've noticed that the male of the species
doesn't respond very well to reason. I wonder if his
responses to all stimuli are as erratic?" Liz gave him
a provocative glance.

"Definitely a bit of research worth pursuing." His
eyes seemed to glow even in the fading light.

Liz glanced once again at the playground, and a
feeling of recklessness swept over her. Her book was
constantly harping about the advantages of doing the
unexpected, wasn't it? So why not add some surprise
to their daily living and not just to their sex life?

"Come on!" She tugged at his arm. "Let's go play on those swings. I haven't been in a playground since the twins were little, and I never got to swing back then. I was always the one who did the pushing."

"You want to swing?" John looked at her as if she'd lost her mind. "In an elegant silk dress and high-heeled sandals? You'll break an ankle."

"No, I won't. You don't swing on your feet. You swing on your rear, and that's in fine shape."

"I'll say it is." John grinned as he gave in and followed her toward the play area.

The mother and son had disappeared, leaving them in total possession of the deserted playground.

Liz sat down on the thick seat of one of the large swings, took a firm grip on the heavy chains, and began to move.

"Give me a push, will you?" she begged John, who was leaning against the end supports.

"I'm tempted," he sighed as he moved in behind her and gave her a gentle shove.

"Higher, John, higher!" Liz leaned her head back and allowed the soft evening breeze to flow over her face. She closed her mind to everything but the wonderful sensation. She felt vitally alive and soaringly free. Right at this moment, life was wonderful. She'd just enjoyed a superb dinner with her husband, she'd practiced her flirting techniques, and when they went back to the hotel, she was going to make love to him. Or he was going to make love to her. Maybe they could take turns. Liz broke into delighted laughter at the thought.

"Liz Langdon!" John grabbed the swing and pulled it to a stop. "You have had too much to drink."

"Do you think so?" She tipped her head back and

stared up into his face. "You could be right. On the other hand, I could simply be drunk on the pleasures of the evening. On the brilliant moon. On the soft breezes. On a sexy man." She reached up and touched his chin. "You, my darling husband, go to my head more quickly than the best brandy."

"It isn't my head that you go to," John said ruefully.

"Hmm." Liz leaned back against his flat stomach. "I see what you mean. So why don't we return to the hotel?" She tilted back farther and rubbed the top of her head over his hard thighs.

"Good idea." He grabbed her arm, hauling her out of the swing. "I'm expecting a call—" he began, then broke off in exasperation as Liz, ignoring what she didn't want to hear, took off.

"Liz, where are you going!"

"I want to whiz down that." She pointed to a huge silver slide.

"You'll break your neck. You might not be drunk, but you're not yourself either."

"I am woman!" She flung her arms outward in a gesture reminiscent of a pagan goddess. "I am eternal woman. I am an enchantress."

"You're nuts." His tone was resigned.

"I am too an enchantress." Liz stomped one small sandaled foot in the reddish dust, inexplicably hurt.

"You're one hot little number," John agreed, "but that doesn't preclude your being nuts."

"You make me sound like an oversexed basket case," Liz objected.

"I'm afraid you'll have to settle for the bathtub," John said with a grin. "There isn't a basket in our sybaritic suite, you licentious woman."

"Licentious." Liz tasted the word. "Yes, I like that. That's exactly how I feel. Licentious. How do you feel?" She peered at him through the darkness.

"Exasperated."

"Oh, poor boy." Liz patted his cheek, and then, unable to help herself, placed a swift kiss on his chin. "I'll tell you what. In the best tradition of modern marriages, we'll compromise."

"Oh?" he replied warily.

"Once down the slide and then we go back to the hotel." She smiled. "And despite what you think, I am not tight. I'm fey. No, pixilated. That's the word."

"Honey, if lady pixies had looked anything like you, the race wouldn't be extinct now. But you'll forgive me if I reserve judgment on the rest of it."

"You reserve judgment, and I'll reserve you," Liz giggled. She began to make her way cautiously up the narrow steps of the large slide, being careful not to catch her heels. She paused as she heard John start up behind her. "Are you coming, too?" she asked, glancing down at him.

"Yes," he sighed. "You're liable to fall off this damn thing."

"Well, if I do, you be sure to catch me." She turned around and continued up.

At the top she paused a second to look around. Then, tucking her skirts around her, she sat down and pushed off. She whizzed to the bottom, laughing all the way. Sitting on the lip of the slide, she turned and looked back up at John.

"Come on down. The water's fine," she teased.

To her surprise, he did, with the same grace of motion he brought to all his activities. Slowing himself down as he approached the bottom, he let his legs slide around her waiting body, and his hard torso hit hers with a gentle bump.

"Nice." Liz wiggled provocatively, wedging herself more firmly between his legs. "I'd forgotten how much fun sliding was." She smiled up into his dark face. "Isn't it amazing what a few embellishments can do?"

"Such as?"

"Oh"—she tipped her head back and lightly began to stroke the back of his neck with her left hand, caressing the firm skin above his collar—"this. Or this." She turned to face him and slipped her right hand inside his jacket and rubbed the palm of her hand over his chest.

"Or this?" John's arms crushed her to him. His mouth fastened hungrily onto her parted lips, and she felt the catch in his breath.

"Mmm." She made a contented sound deep in her throat and reached up to hug his straining body closer.

A brilliant flare of light shocked her dilated pupils, and she jerked backward in protest as the security guard's light moved over her. Swinging back up, it illuminated John's furious features.

"Put that damn thing down!" John bit out.

"Sorry, Senator," the guard apologized. "I didn't realize it was you." He paused awkwardly. "If you don't need anything, I'll just be going."

"Do that!" John's voice held uncompromising dismissal, and with a nervous nod the shadowy figure moved off.

Liz waited until the man had reached the parking lot and then whispered to John, "Who on earth do you suppose he thought you were?"

"God only knows," John whispered back, laughter

coloring his tone. "I'm not up enough on politics to know which of our hardworking senators is in the habit of cavorting with beautiful women in playgrounds."

"Considering some of the things a few senators have done, this hardly seems worth mentioning." She allowed John to lift her to her feet.

"Then we'll have to rehearse a little," he said. "I'd hate to think that what I was just doing came under the category of hardly worth mentioning."

"Hardly," Liz giggled as she followed along beside him. It had been a lovely night, and it wasn't over yet. Not by a long shot. She could sense John's puzzlement over her unusually flirtatious behavior, but that didn't bother her. The book had been very specific about the dangers of being taken for granted, as well as the necessity of keeping him off-balance. John was certainly off-balance, Liz thought with a satisfied smile. And she hadn't even hit her stride yet. An anticipatory smile claimed her lips as she climbed into their rented car.

"After you, my lady." John swung open the door to their suite and motioned her in.

Liz frowned, remembering the bookstore poster showing the luscious man with the equally luscious woman clasped to his manly chest. She leaned into John and tried smiling seductively.

Instead of sweeping her up into his arms and carrying her into the bedroom the way he was supposed to, he put his hands around her waist and gently pushed her into the room.

"Are you all right? You've been acting strange all night."

"Strange!" Liz glared at him, furious at hearing her attempts at seductive behavior described as strange. She opened her mouth to give him a pithy description of just what she thought of his choice of adjectives, but he turned and moved away.

"Why don't you take a shower while I check with the desk for messages?"

Liz swallowed her hasty words, reminded of her plans. She'd take a bath and then have a go at seducing him. Mentally she considered the black negligee she'd packed. If that didn't give him ideas, he was hopeless. She started toward the bedroom, knowing John would be on the telephone for several minutes.

"Fine, I'll meet you in the bar." John's voice caught her attention, and she turned back.

He hung up the phone and stared thoughtfully at the wall, his dark eyebrows knit, his face a mask of absorbed concentration.

Liz's heart sank. She knew that expression. Something or someone had captured his attention. She doubted he even remembered she was there.

"John?" she asked tentatively, failing to rouse him from his musing. "John!" she repeated more strongly.

He blinked and then glanced absently at her. "Sorry, darling, I have to run downstairs for a while."

"Oh, John," Liz wailed, "do you have to?"

"Yes, I do." He dropped a kiss on her brow. "I'm meeting two men I've been corresponding with. It's important."

More important than making love to your wife? The angry words formed in her mind, but she knew her disappointment was making her unreasonable. She knew John had come to Washington to work, not to entertain her. If she persisted in demanding his presence, he was going to regret ever having agreed to bring her. Drawing on years of practice, Liz forced down her frustrations. After all, he'd told her where he was going and why, and that was more than he usually did.

"Fine." She gave him a smile that wavered slightly around the edges. "I think you were right about my having had too much to drink. I'll go to bed."

"Do that." John patted her shoulder, his mind clearly elsewhere. "I'll try not to wake you when I return."

Liz tried to be philosophical as he left. You couldn't win them all. But at least she hadn't entirely struck out. The memory of the evening cheered her, as did the thought that she and John still had two more nights away from home.

9

"IMPRESSIVE GATHERING, isn't it?" Carol leaned closer to Liz.

"Uh-huh," Liz agreed with a rueful grimace. "I feel faintly suffocated under the weight of so much dignity."

"You can say that again." Carol glanced around the packed auditorium. "I haven't seen this many three-piece suits since we went to the fire sale at that clothing factory last year."

"Shh," Liz hushed her, "someone will hear."

"Nonsense," Carol scoffed. "From the bored expressions on their faces, I doubt they're hearing anything. Look at that one over there." She pointed to a woman seated about five rows in front of them. "She looks like an experiment that failed."

"Carol!" A gurgle of laughter escaped Liz. "She's probably a very competent, dedicated pediatrician."

"And doesn't she know it. She looks as if she's trying on halos. What is it about the medical profession that turns perfectly normal people into sanctimonious stuffed shirts?"

"Quit generalizing." Liz's gaze swept the noisy auditorium again. "Aren't they ever going to start?"

"Have you ever known a doctor to be on time?" Carol replied sardonically. "Why on earth I let you drag me to this lecture I'll never know."

"Because underneath that glossy exterior of yours beats a heart of mush." Liz grinned at her. "You know I want to hear John's speech, and I wouldn't have had the courage to come by myself. Everyone can tell just by looking at me that I don't really belong."

"I'll say," Carol cheerfully agreed with a speculative look at Liz's bronze linen Chanel-cut suit and brightly patterned silk blouse. "No doctor ever looked that good."

Liz nervously rubbed a damp palm over the nubby texture of her skirt. "It is nice, isn't it?"

"It's not nice; it's spectacular."

"Thank you. I wish they'd start." Liz shifted restlessly.

"Me, too," Carol agreed. "The sooner they start, the sooner we can cut out of here. What time did John say he was scheduled to speak?"

"He didn't," Liz replied, not mentioning that he hadn't been there to ask. She'd been asleep when he finally returned to the suite last night, and he was already gone when she awakened that morning. If it hadn't been for the note he'd left, telling her he'd be tied up in meetings until five-thirty and to enjoy her day, she wouldn't have been certain he'd returned at all. She bit her lip as she considered that brief missive. It hadn't contained a word about her coming to hear him give his speech, even though she'd told him she wanted to.

Maybe he hadn't wanted her to come. Or maybe he simply hadn't been listening to her when she said it. She pressed her lips together. Well, it was too bad if he didn't want her present, because she was here, and here she was going to stay. This was one aspect of his professional life she could share, and she was determined to do so.

At least he wasn't likely to see her, sequestered as she was in the back row. That way, if he muffed his speech, she could always pretend not to know what had happened. The thought of his possible failure made her stomach lurch, and she swallowed uneasily. She couldn't have been more nervous if she'd been scheduled to give the keynote address herself.

"Finally," Carol said in exaggerated relief as the moderator walked to the podium.

Liz leaned forward to hear the man's short welcoming speech, which ended with his introduction of John.

"Will you look at him?" one of the two young women seated directly in front of Liz and Carol whispered audibly to her companion. "He can practice his bedside manner on me anytime."

"You should be so lucky," her friend retorted.

"Who is he anyway?"

Liz leaned forward and held her breath, frankly eavesdropping.

"A very fast-rising star from New York State. My friend on the steering committee tells me rumor has it that..."

Liz willed the woman to finish her sentence. Rumor

said what? But to her frustration, John replaced the moderator on the podium, and with a hissed, "Later," to her companion, the woman gave him her undivided attention.

Thwarted, Liz looked up at her husband. A husband she barely recognized in this setting. His superbly tailored three-piece gray suit fit him to perfection, outlining the lean strength of his body. His white shirt was spotless, and his maroon silk tie added just the right understated accent. But it wasn't just the clothes that created the impression of John's being someone special.

Liz tried to analyze the aura surrounding him. It emanated from the man himself—from the gleaming smile he gave the audience, from his calm, competent manner as he began to speak. He looked and sounded exactly like what he was: a highly skilled, distinguished member of the medical profession.

Liz leaned back, closed her eyes, and let his resonant voice flow over her, soothing her frayed nerves. She could have laughed at how worried she'd been for him, at how concerned she'd been that he might not do as well as he wanted to. He was perfectly capable of handling this speech on his own.

The thought depressed her. He didn't even need her as a cheering section. He already had that. Liz glanced sourly at the two young women in front of her, both of whom were hanging on his every word.

An amused ripple of laughter greeted one of John's remarks, and Liz quickly corralled her attention back to what he was saying.

Unfortunately, it proved to be a lesson in futility. She listened with mounting frustration as the unfamiliar words rolled right over her head.

Frowning, she glanced around. Carol was reading a lurid-looking paperback, but no one else seemed to be having any trouble understanding what John was saying. In fact, they all looked fascinated. And while Liz was willing to bet that the two women in front of her were more interested in the man than in his words, that could hardly hold true for the entire audience. What he was saying was apparently fascinating to those who had the background and the intelligence to decipher it.

A quake of dejection shook her as she faced the undeniable fact that she didn't. She couldn't begin to comprehend the more abstruse details of his work, let alone intelligently discuss them with him. She felt like bursting into tears. How frustrating it must be for John to have to rephrase everything so she could understand him. No wonder he'd quit talking to her about his work, she thought on a rising tide of panic. How on earth could she ever hope to hold the interest of such a highly intellectual man? Especially when her own abilities were so depressingly normal.

For a second the very real fear that she'd already lost him engulfed her, and she felt sickeningly faint before her natural common sense gained ascendancy. She was overreacting, she firmly told herself.

So what if she wasn't John's intellectual equal? She never had been, and he'd married her anyway. That thought provided a ray of sunlight, which she doggedly pursued. If John had wanted a brilliant wife with a career to rival his own, he could have found one. There had certainly been enough women after him when they were going together. And at least one since. The thought of Brandy Rome crossed her mind.

He'd chosen to marry her, lack of knowledge and

all, Liz told herself. Maybe she was missing the point regarding his work. Perhaps instead of trying to discuss it with him, she should concentrate more on being a good listener. After all, John had scores of colleagues to discuss his work with, but few of them would have either the time or the inclination to simply listen without professional prejudice.

Yes, she decided, that was undoubtedly her most viable option: to continue to be a good listener and to save her attempts at actual discussion for nonmedical matters. In those she was already making progress, she encouraged herself. John was beginning to respond to her overtures. She mentally listed her small accomplishments: his telling her where he was going when he'd left last night, as well as his sharing several things that had happened at work earlier in the week.

Taken by themselves they weren't much, but she had to start somewhere. At least John was beginning to talk to her again. It was up to her now to do her best to protect that fragile new link between them.

But there was a much stronger tie that bound them together, she acknowledged with satisfaction—a tie that had developed over the years into a thread of steel. And that was their physical pleasure in each other. Granted she'd allowed the expression of that pleasure to slip into the commonplace, but she'd already taken steps to remedy that. And with a great deal of success. A contented smile curved her lips at the memory of yesterday's interlude in the bathtub.

Perhaps she ought to concentrate her efforts more on welding their physical compatibility into an unbreakable bond and forget about changing her image. Especially since John actually seemed to prefer suburban housewife to femme fatale.

She cast her mind back over the book's chapter on adding spice to one's sex life, her heart beating a little more quickly as she recalled one particularly outrageous suggestion. The hotel would be the perfect place to try it. She wouldn't have to worry about the boys appearing unexpectedly. She'd do it. All she needed was to find a grocery store before John got back to the suite tonight . . .

A sharp burst of applause cut into her thoughts, and she automatically joined in as John left the podium.

"Satisfied now?" Carol asked airily, shoving her book into her capacious purse.

"Yes," Liz replied tentatively. Then, unable to help herself, she asked, "Did you understand any of it?"

"Of course not."

"Good." Liz smiled in relief. "It's nice to know I have company in my stupidity."

"Lack of particular knowledge in a given field can hardly be construed as stupidity!" Carol protested.

Liz grinned at her friend's reassuring pragmatism. "Okay, calm down, and let's go shopping," she pacified. "I have to be back by five at the very latest."

"Don't worry. John will be late anyway," Carol confidently predicted. "Doctors always are. Some earnest, bespectacled type is bound to corner him to discuss his speech."

"Along with some not so earnest, bespectacled types," Liz commented wryly, her eyes drawn to the two young women who had sat in front of her. She could see them making their way up the crowded aisle toward the podium, where John stood talking to a group of people. She never did find out what rumor said, but maybe it was better that way. She had more problems than she could handle at the moment. She didn't need anything else to worry about.

"Come on, Liz," Carol prodded her. "I want to go down to Wisconsin Avenue and check out the shops."

"Coming." Liz picked up her purse and followed Carol out. "Where will they all go now?" she asked curiously with a backward glance at the milling crowd.

"Committee meetings, lectures, seminars, that kind of thing. Forget about them and concentrate on shopping."

"Okay." Liz made an effort to be a good companion. "I want to pick up a few surprises for the boys anyway."

"You and those kids!" Carol groaned. "As gung ho as you are, I'm surprised you and John don't have a dozen."

"Maybe we would if I could ever count on his being home!" Liz blurted.

"You forgot to say 'It serves him right,'" Carol said cheerfully.

"What?" Liz frowned at her friend.

"Your tone of voice," Carol explained. "Just like when we were kids, and we'd get mad and yell at each other. We'd always finish up by saying, 'It serves you right!' Hurry up, there's a taxi just dropping someone off. Let's grab it." She pulled Liz through the door.

Liz stumbled blindly into the taxi as Carol's words ricocheted through her mind. *It serves him right. It serves him right.* The phrase beat into her brain. She instinctively denied the unavoidable conclusion. It wasn't true. She hadn't been refusing to have another child to punish John for being so engrossed in his work. Had she?

Limp with dismay, she sank back into the taxi's worn vinyl seat and stared blankly out the window, letting Carol's happy chatter flow past her. It wasn't true, she insisted. Only a horrible, vengeful person could do something like that. Or a desperate one. One who hoped that by tying her refusal to have another child to her husband's long working hours, she might force him to cut down on his work load.

Oh, dear God! She bit her lip. What had she done? Had she really tried to use John's love of children as a weapon to force him to conform to her need to have him home more?

Somehow the fact that she'd been acting subconsciously seemed to make it even worse—as if she were so ashamed of her actions that she couldn't acknowledge them, even in her own mind. Until one careless remark of Carol's had forced her to face them.

"Out!" Carol poked her. "I've already paid the driver, and I suspect he'd like to go elsewhere."

"Certainly." Liz made a determined effort to pull herself together as she stumbled out onto the sidewalk.

"Liz?" Carol was frowning at her. "Liz, what is it with you? You've been acting weird ever since last week in Sibley's. Changing your hairdo, buying new clothes, walking around in a fog. You're too old for puberty and too young for menopause, so for heaven's sake, what's wrong?"

Liz heard the concern lurking behind Carol's characteristic brusqueness, but her own thoughts were too frenzied to share with even the most intimate of confidantes. "I'm just getting in touch with the real me," she lied.

"All right, so don't tell me. Even I can take a hint if it's repeated often enough. I'll mind my own business. Come on. Let's start on this side of the street and work our way back on the other."

Carol looked unconvinced by Liz's blatant side-stepping of the issue, but Liz was grateful her friend had simply changed the subject. "Okay," she readily agreed. "As long as I get back by five."

It was actually five-ten by the time Liz returned to the hotel. To her relief their suite was empty. John was apparently still tied up in meetings. That gave her twenty minutes to turn herself into a raving sex goddess. A happy gurgle of laughter escaped her as she pictured the expression on John's face when he opened the door.

"John Langdon, you aren't going to know what hit you," she vowed. "You're going to think you wandered into an X-rated sexual fantasy."

A subdued bong from the Cupid-encrusted clock marked the quarter-hour, propelling her into action, and she hurried into the bath. Bypassing the tub, she took a quick shower and toweled herself dry before reaching for the roll of plastic wrap.

Liz looked at her image in the mirror over the vanity and then glanced down at the roll in her hand. Exactly how did one put on a cellophane bikini? The book hadn't included any specifics beyond the basic idea.

It would probably stick to itself, she finally decided. It did when she used it on food. "Just pretend you're an onion," she muttered. She promptly burst into lighthearted laughter.

Her first attempt was too tight, and the bikini split when she tried to move. Her second try was more satisfactory. She used a longer piece, wrapped it loosely around herself, and then tucked the ends under.

Critically she examined the results. It certainly was sexy. Different, too. That, she recalled, was supposed to be half of the secret of its success. The element of surprise. After all, it wasn't every day that a man was greeted at the door by a woman wearing a transparent bikini, a seductive smile, and nothing else. Not that the wrap would stay on long, knowing John and his recently reactivated randiness. Her eyes took on a dreamy, faraway look.

A second bong announced the half-hour, and Liz hastily ran her fingers through her curls and splashed on some of John's favorite scent. To get the maximum effect from this outfit, she had to meet him at the door.

A cautious peek into the living room showed her it was still empty, and she flitted across to the door, securing the safety chain. She was willing to bet John had left his key somewhere, but she didn't intend to take any chances.

She then wandered over to the sofa and attempted to sit down, but an ominous crackle made her think better of the idea. Instead, she began to pace between the door and the window, praying he wouldn't be late. The air conditioning, which had felt so heavenly when she'd first come in from outside, now felt like a blast right off the Arctic Circle.

She rubbed her hands over the goose bumps on her arms and shivered. She was about to find a blanket to wrap around herself when she heard the sound of the door handle turning.

John! Her breath caught, and her abdomen tightened in excitement. She hurried to the door.

"Just a minute, darling," she called. She unfastened

the chain and was about to unlock the door when her natural sense of caution asserted itself. Wanting to make sure there was no one passing in the hall, she peered through the peephole, blinked, and then looked again.

John had two men with him! Her mental processes froze, and she stared blankly at the door.

"Liz?" John called.

"Oh, damn!" she groaned. "Damn! Damn! Damn!" She'd never even considered this possibility.

"Just a second!" she yelled as she flew toward the bedroom in a frantic search for clothes. She flung open the bureau door, breaking a fingernail in the process. She tugged at the plastic wrap with one hand, but it didn't budge, and she could have screamed in frustration. Just her luck! She'd managed to get the kind of wrap that really worked instead of a cheap imitation.

An imperative knock on the door echoed through the suite, and with a despairing whimper she pulled on a pair of jeans and a yellow turtleneck. Not bothering to look for shoes, she sped back toward the living room.

She winced as she caught a glimpse of herself in one of the many bedroom mirrors. Her hair was flying every which way, her feet were bare, and the neck of her jersey had devoured her chin and was advancing on her ears. She yanked the constricting collar down and took a deep breath. There was no hope for it. She would have to let the visitors in and try to act as if she always greeted her husband's colleagues looking like something out of Dogpatch. Her only consolation was that neither of the men with John had looked familiar; she could hope she'd never see them again after today.

She swung the door open just as John was about to knock again.

"Hi." She smiled weakly at the trio. "Sorry about the delay. I was just..." Her voice trailed off, as she was unable to think of a good lie on the spur of the moment. "Come in." She moved aside to allow them to enter.

"Hi, darling." John dropped a kiss on her cheek and, putting a comforting arm around her shoulders, turned her to face the men.

Liz allowed her tense body to relax slightly against John's, attempting to draw confidence from him. This was nothing to be upset about, she told herself. Lots of women were caught unawares when their husbands brought home colleagues. At least she wasn't expected to feed them!

"Liz, I'd like you to meet Dr. Jason Irving and Dr. Neil Tinsdale. They're from Cambridge."

"How do you do?" Liz automatically responded.

"Mrs. Langdon." The elder of the two, Dr. Tinsdale, a courtly gentleman of about sixty with a snow-white beard and mustache, smiled gently at her, his bright blue eyes twinkling.

"Have a seat while I get you all a drink," John directed.

Liz followed the two strangers across the room. She sank down on the sofa across from them, suddenly remembering the plastic wrap when it crackled protestingly at the movement.

Her eyes widened at the sound, and she glanced apprehensively at the visitors. Her hope that they hadn't heard was dashed by the faintly puzzled expression on the face of the younger doctor, Jason Irving.

Hoping to divert his attention, Liz said quickly, "Are you a pediatrician, too, Dr. Irving?" She immediately winced at the inanity of the remark. Of all the dumb questions to ask a participant at a pediatrics convention.

"Yes." He nodded gravely. "I specialize in child psychiatry."

"Oh?" Liz replied weakly, not liking the way he was eyeing her. Fortunately, John brought the drinks, which served to distract Dr. Irving.

"Here you are, Liz." He handed her a glass of white wine.

She reached for it, her hand stopping in midair as another ominous crackle resonated through the air. Gritting her teeth, Liz grabbed the slender wineglass stem, trying to ignore the noise. She peeked up at John, but he continued to hand out drinks, seemingly unaware of her dilemma. She frowned. John might be absentminded at times, but usually he wasn't unobservant. Unless his mind was totally preoccupied with other things. Such as his two guests? She looked back at the pair on the sofa only to find the young psychiatrist's gimlet eyes fixed on her. Just who were these two men? And how important were they to John? And why? They weren't even from the same state.

"Do you work, Mrs. Langdon?" the psychiatrist asked.

"Yes," Liz replied coolly, surprising even herself, "I just don't get paid for it."

"Oh, you stay at home?" His condescending smile set her teeth on edge.

"I'm not there now, am I?" Liz smiled back.

She watched the corners of the older man's mouth disappear upward into his mustache, and she began to feel better. At least one of the two had a sense of humor. As it turned out, Dr. Tinsdale also had an excellent sense of his duties as a guest.

Taking the conversation firmly into his competent hands, the older man focused it on convention matters, which allowed Liz to sink back into the sofa and try to regain her equilibrium. After what seemed like an interminable thirty minutes, the two men finally finished their drinks and got up to go.

Liz stood to the accompaniment of loud crackles, too pleased that they were leaving to care that the psychiatrist was eyeing her as if she were a prospective patient. She said her good-byes with a heartfelt relief that she hoped wasn't too evident. She really rather liked Dr. Tinsdale.

Once the door had closed firmly behind the pair, John turned to her. "What's the matter, Liz? You weren't your usual friendly self."

Liz glared at him as a wave of helpless self-pity washed over her. Not her usual friendly self! How in heaven's name could he expect her to be her usual friendly self when she was swathed in cellophane that crackled every time she moved? When she was barefoot and trying not to notice that a psychiatrist was studying her as if she were some new psychotic type he was planning to write a paper on? To her horror, she burst into tears, surprising herself as much as John.

"Liz!" He sounded appalled. "Don't cry. I wasn't criticizing you."

He swiftly crossed the room and, scooping her up in his arms, sat down on the sofa. He cradled her body against his chest and gently rocked her back and forth.

"Don't cry, darling Liz. Don't cry, love." He placed comforting kisses on her damp cheek.

"I'm sorry," Liz hiccuped. "It was just—" She gulped. "I wasn't expecting...It was the bikini."

"Bikini?" He pushed her back against his supporting arm and began to stroke her tangled curls off her hot, flushed face. "You bought a bikini?" he encouraged her.

"No." Liz gulped again. "I mean...Well, you see, I read about..." She paused and then burst out, "I was going to greet you at the door wearing a cellophane bikini, a seductive smile, and nothing else, and then, when you brought those men along, I had to jump into the first thing I could find."

"So that's why you took so long to open the door." His voice wavered.

"And I crackled when I moved," Liz wailed, "and that blasted psychiatrist kept watching me."

To her utter fury, John burst into unrestrained laughter.

"John Langdon!" she shouted at him. "It wasn't funny. It was humiliating. Don't you dare laugh!" she protested as he continued to roar with unrestrained mirth.

Madder than she'd been in years, she grabbed one of the heart-shaped pillows from the sofa and began to beat him over the head with it.

"Liz!" He grabbed her wrist and pulled her down on the cushions, then rolled on top of her, trapping her flailing limbs beneath his lean but substantial body. "Calm down. I'm sorry I laughed, but..." His lips twitched, and she felt a quiver shake his body.

He firmed his mouth and went on. "It was a lovely idea, and I'm sorry I spoiled it." He deposited a tiny kiss on her red nose. "I've never seen a cellophane bikini before."

Liz peered suspiciously into his obsidian eyes, which were alight with the laughter he was trying hard to hide. A reluctant smile teased her mouth.

"I guess it was kind of funny," she conceded.

"Poor angel." He began to nibble on her ear. "Tomorrow I promise faithfully I'll come back alone, and you can surprise me, hmm?" His lips wandered down to her neck.

"It's a deal." Liz wriggled beneath him, drawing satisfaction from the immediate reaction of his body.

"But for now," he sighed regretfully, "we're meeting Carol and Gary for dinner in twenty minutes, and, knowing them, if we don't show up, they'll come looking for us."

"We could just not answer the door and hope they'll go away." Liz let her fingers slip under his belt and inch toward the elastic waistband of his shorts.

"Do you really think that would stop Carol?" John asked sardonically.

"No," she sighed reluctantly as he stood up. "But just you wait until tomorrow, John Langdon."

"With bated breath . . . to say nothing of the rest of me," he said, pulling her to her feet.

10

"HELLO?" LIZ MUTTERED sleepily into the pink phone.

"Liz?" Carol's strident voice demanded. "Is that you?"

"No, it's not me."

"For heaven's sake, wake up, Liz. It's eleven o'clock. How could you still be asleep?"

It was easy, providing you'd spent the night as she had. She burrowed deeper into the sleek pink satin sheets. The plastic wrap had been a definite success. A supremely satisfied smile curved her kiss-swollen lips.

"Liz, don't you dare go back to sleep on me!"

"Why not?" Liz yawned.

"Because our husbands' meeting was canceled at the last minute, and they're free until almost two."

"Oh?" Liz began to wake up, envisioning a whole host of delightful possibilities. Possibilities Carol promptly dashed with her next words.

"And I got them to agree to take us to the Smithsonian. John wanted to have a quick word with someone, so I said I'd roust you out of bed."

"The Smithsonian?" Liz repeated incredulously. "You want to visit a museum? Since when?"

"Since I found out about the jewel collection housed there." Carol seemed unperturbed by her friend's disbelief in her interest in things cultural.

"That explains it," Liz laughed.

"So hurry up! We don't have any time to waste. This is our only chance to go. I'd hate to head home tonight without having seen those gems."

"Okay, I'll come, but only on the condition that I get to see the moon rock."

"Moon rock?"

"To each his own. The boys will want to know all about it."

"You and those kids," Carol good-naturedly complained. "All right, but hurry up, because we won't wait for you."

"John will," Liz teased. Then she relented. "Give me fifteen minutes, and I'll meet you downstairs."

In actuality it was twenty minutes later when she joined the trio in the lobby.

"You're late," Carol accused.

"But it was worth the wait," a masculine voice intoned. Admiration gleamed deep in John's dark eyes as he caressingly studied the dark rose blouson dress Liz was wearing. His gaze lingered on the firm swell of her breasts outlined against the thin silk, and Liz felt a familiar rush of warmth flood her body. She moistened her lips as her eyes met his in perfect understanding. He knew what she was remembering. Knew and approved.

Drat Carol and her jewels anyway! She didn't really

want to be dragged off to gape at a bunch of colored rocks. Not when she and John could be doing other things. This would be their last chance to be alone for a while, she sighed in regret. They were scheduled to fly back to Rochester an hour after John's last meeting today.

But what could she say to Carol and Gary? Please excuse us, but I'd much rather make love to my husband than go with you? She tried the words out in her mind but found she lacked the courage to say them aloud.

"That honeymoon suite's starting to get to you two," Carol guessed. "Look at you, standing there looking deep into each other's eyes. Come on." She grabbed Gary's arm and hurried toward the door.

"Were you able to get some sleep?" John asked as they followed the pair.

"Uh-huh." Liz slipped a hand into the crook of his arm and briefly hugged him to her. "But what about you, you poor man?" She searched his dear face anxiously, but to her relief he seemed more relaxed than he'd been in ages.

"You can keep me up all night like that any time you want to," he chuckled. "I haven't felt so refreshed in ages."

Liz felt a warm glow envelop her at his words. It was working! At least one segment of her plan was beginning to show definite signs of success. She sighed happily. If she'd realized just how much depth a little imagination could add to their lovemaking, she'd have tried it years ago.

Maybe she'd even read that author Carol had been so keen on. Bliss . . . Liz searched her memory. Bliss Storm. That was it. Something about love in the sand.

She'd definitely read it, she decided as John helped her into their rented car.

"Where's the museum?" Carol demanded as John swung the car into a huge city parking garage.

"According to the desk clerk at the hotel, parking in the museum mall is almost impossible. So we'll leave the car here and walk the five blocks."

"Walk!" Carol repeated incredulously from the back seat. "Walk five blocks?"

"Come off it, Carol," Liz said. "I'll bet you walked ten miles through those stores yesterday, to say nothing of the day before."

"But that was shopping," Carol wailed.

"So pretend you're going to buy something," Liz helpfully suggested.

"That's not going to help," Carol muttered, climbing out of the car.

Liz ignored her friend as she dug into her brown leather purse and extracted her guidebook.

"Oh, no!" Carol stopped complaining long enough to object in mock agony. "I refuse to listen to that book again. Do you know," she demanded of Gary, "that Liz spent ages Friday reading to me about Georgetown?"

"Interrupted your concentration on shopping, did she?" Gary asked blandly.

"I thought you were the one who was always advocating education, Carol," Liz teased.

"Only in the abstract." Gary laughed while Carol subsided into feeble mutters.

"There! There's the castle!" Liz's enthusiasm for sight-seeing heightened when they actually arrived on the mall.

"That's where the moon rock is." Gary pointed at

another building to their right. "Why don't we see it first, view the jewel collection, and then grab a quick lunch?"

In agreement they entered the building and joined the short line of people waiting to see the lunar stone.

When her turn came, Liz blinked down at the rock encased in a glass dome. "But it's only a plain grayish rock," she complained.

"What did you expect?" Carol teased. "Trumpets and a brass band?"

Liz groped to explain her disappointment. "It looks so—so ordinary. It came all the way from the moon, and yet, if you dropped it on the ground, you couldn't tell it from the other rocks. It should look as special as it is."

"Maybe you could convince NASA to spray it with gold paint for you." Carol tweaked her.

"You have no imagination," Liz accused.

"And you have too much," Carol playfully retaliated. "Forget that cinder, and let's go see the Hope Diamond. That's one rock I guarantee you won't be disappointed in."

Minutes later Liz again found herself in front of a rock exhibit.

"So that's what the world's largest blue diamond looks like." Liz peered down at it.

"All forty-four and a half carats of it," John answered.

"Now *that* is a rock I can relate to," Carol breathed in awe as she stared at it.

"As long as you relate from a distance," Gary warned. "It's got a curse on it."

"A curse?" Carol laughed. "You can't seriously believe in curses!"

"He's got a point," Liz told her. "According to my guidebook, ever since it was smuggled out of India in the seventeenth century, many of its owners have been plagued with bad luck or have died violent deaths. I wouldn't have it even as a gift. But that blue thing is nice." She indicated the next exhibit.

"That blue thing, my dear, happens to be a four-hundred-carat sapphire," John said dryly.

"Too ostentatious," Liz decided with a sigh of regret. "No one would ever believe it was real."

"Oh, look at that!" A tray of black pearls caught Carol's attention, and she moved closer to them. "Aren't they gorgeous?"

Carol's admiration didn't really require an answer, and Liz didn't attempt one, content to linger beside John while Carol and Gary worked their way around the room.

"Do we have time to see anything else?" Liz asked once Carol had finally looked her fill. "We could see the original Star-Spangled Banner, or maybe George Washington's false teeth."

"My God," Gary intoned, "is nothing sacred?"

"Sorry, darling." John sounded regretful. "We should be heading back if we're going to be on time for this afternoon's session. We'll return for a long weekend later in the year and bring the boys with us. They'd love George Washington's false teeth."

"I'll hold you to it." Liz took heart from his suggestion. He'd never offered to take her and the boys away before. Maybe it had been a spur-of-the-moment idea, but he'd still had it. It was one more small success for her campaign.

Liz blinked as they walked out into the bright September sunshine, and the hot, humid air hit her like a blow. Fall had not even begun to arrive in Washington, D.C.

"You may not be able to park on the mall," Carol observed, looking around the crowded streets, "but driving doesn't seem to be a problem."

"So?" Liz asked.

"So let's wait here while the men go get the car and come back for us. My feet are killing me." She held out one shapely foot in its high-heeled sandal.

Liz forbore to point out that Carol hadn't had any trouble with her feet yesterday when she'd shopped for six consecutive hours. Instead she eagerly grasped at her friend's suggestion to gain a few minutes alone with John.

"You poor thing," Liz sympathized. "You and Gary wait here while John and I go get the car."

"That's okay, Liz," Gary interjected. "I'll go with John. You can stay with Carol."

"Don't be dense, Gary," Carol said. "They want to be alone."

"Right in one." Liz grabbed John's arm and hurried him away.

"Did you enjoy yourself?" John asked.

"Yes." She smiled happily at him, more pleased by his physical presence than by what she'd seen. "I'm so glad I came to Washington with you."

"Me, too." John briefly hugged her to him. "I never realized just how much fun a convention could be."

"You, sir, are a full-fledged lecher."

"Full-fledged? You flatter me!"

"Actually you flatter me." Liz grinned. "Among other things. What's your meeting about this afternoon?"

"Emotionally induced asthma," he replied with his

usual brevity. But this time, to her unbounded delight, he began to elaborate on the subject, tying it to a particularly frustrating case he was working on.

Remembering her resolve to be a good listener, Liz gave him her total attention, interrupting only to ask a question when she didn't quite understand what he was saying. It wasn't a subject that greatly interested her, but the fact that John had introduced it without a great deal of prodding on her part encouraged her immensely.

It was another thin filament in the frail thread of substantive communication she was trying to spin. Being alone with John away from the horrendous demands of his patients had been an excellent idea. Now all that remained was to be careful that, once back home, John didn't slip into his habit of shutting her out.

"I'll walk you to your meeting before I go upstairs," Liz offered once they were back at the hotel.

"Are you going anywhere this afternoon?" John asked.

"It wouldn't be worth it. We have to leave for the airport by four-thirty at the latest, and it's almost two now. I thought I'd take one last soak in that incredible tub and then pack our bags."

"I wish you hadn't told me that," he groaned. "How am I supposed to concentrate on asthma when I know you're lying in that bathtub? The warm water moving slowly over your sleek skin, slipping over your soft stomach, caressing your lush breasts, creeping into all the secret places of your magnificent body . . ."

"John!" Liz felt her breathing quicken at the visual picture he was creating. "Stop it. I'm going to spend the whole afternoon wanting you."

"Good." He was clearly unrepentant. "Why should I suffer alone when we can be frustrated together?"

"Just concentrate on being a dedicated doctor," Liz suggested, grinning.

"My mind might be dedicated to my profession, but my body is dedicated to you."

"That's the way it should be."

They stopped in front of the door John had been seeking.

She reached up to kiss his cheek. "I love you, John Langdon."

"Liz..." He rubbed the back of his knuckles over her soft cheek in a gentle caress, but a slight frown creased his forehead.

"What's wrong?"

The uncertain look on his face vanished, and he smiled at her. "Absolutely nothing. I'll see you in a couple of hours."

Liz watched him move purposefully into the crowded room before she turned to leave. The supremely contented glow that was the result of last night's lovemaking still held her in thrall.

She stepped into the elevator and pushed the button for the third floor. Minutes later she was back in their suite. A regretful sigh escaped her as she glanced around the room. Much as she wanted to go home to the twins, she was still reluctant to leave. She and John had had such a delightful three days here. They had finally found the time to explore each other both physically and mentally as they hadn't in years.

All good things come to an end, she told herself. You had a wonderful time, but now you must return to the real world. She'd had much more than a wonderful time, she acknowledged. Not only had she advanced her campaign to revitalize her marriage, but she'd also managed to dispel the specter of Brandy Rome once and for all.

Her rational side might have always known that Brandy was not a threat to her, but now her heart knew it, too. Brandy's sole function had been to shock Liz into facing the problems in her marriage. And in facing them, Liz had gained the courage to do something about them. For that, Brandy deserved her heartfelt thanks, Liz admitted. If she hadn't seen the younger woman in John's arms, who knew how long she might have allowed the unsatisfactory state of her marriage to continue?

No, despite Brandy's efforts to the contrary, Liz doubted that John had ever seen his temporary secretary as a desirable woman. For some reason Liz didn't fully understand, she herself held all of his love. A love she intended to keep, she vowed. To keep and to nurture. She'd laid the foundation on which she wanted their marriage to grow; now all she had to do was continue to build on it.

"Just coffee, Liz. I haven't got time for breakfast." John dropped his brown leather briefcase on the kitchen counter, picked up a tumbler of orange juice, and drained it.

"I've got to get in early today. I want to see the O'Reillys before Michael goes in for surgery." He accepted a cup of coffee from her and pressed a light kiss on her lips in exchange.

"Michael?" Liz murmured.

"I told you about him last week, the day after we got back from Washington."

"I remember, the little boy with the cleft palate."

Contrary to her initial worries, John had continued to talk to her. Just not as often or in as much depth as she could have wished. But the problem wasn't an unwillingness on his part. The problem was that since they had returned, John had spent exactly half of one evening at home. Except for a snatched hour here and there, she and the boys had rarely seen him. But some of those hours had been memorable. A reminiscent smile curved her lips.

"What are you thinking about?" John pulled her into his arms and began to softly tongue her ear.

"That," Liz laughed, turning around and insinuating her arms into the loose confines of his suit jacket. "And this." She slid her body sensuously along his lean frame.

"Mmm," he sighed, "you have the nicest thoughts." His hands slipped down to her hips, lifting her against the hard shape of him. "The rest of you isn't too bad either." His mouth sought hers.

Her lips parted beneath his probing tongue, welcoming the sensual invasion. Her eyes slid shut, and she made no attempt to hide her reaction to him. She wanted him. Wanted him with an elemental hunger that seemed to have grown since their trip to Washington.

With a sigh of regret that echoed her own feelings, John put her down. "It's a good thing it's a ten-minute drive to the hospital," he said, grinning at her. "It'll give me time to get back to normal."

"You mean this isn't normal?" Liz opened her eyes in mock astonishment. "And here I thought you were always a sex maniac."

"I'm trying," he laughed, grabbing his briefcase.

"Get a baby-sitter for the boys tomorrow night, and I'll take you out to dinner."

"What time?" Liz called after him.

"About seven," his voice floated back, and Liz smiled happily, already anticipating the evening. She glanced down at the sandwiches she was making and frowned as a nagging problem intruded into her thoughts.

Fretfully, she brushed the bread crumbs off the counter, wishing she could sweep her own thoughts away so cleanly. But her dilemma remained, and sometime soon she was going to have to do something about it. But what could she say to John? "I suddenly realized that the real reason I've been refusing to have another child was because I was getting even with you for not being at home more? Not only that, but I was actually jealous of the time you spent with the boys?" Hardly. It made her sound totally selfish.

So what was she to do? Liz deftly sliced the sandwiches and slipped them into the twins' lunch boxes. Just get pregnant? But that seemed so underhanded. Like . . .

"Mom, Jaimie took my tie just because he flushed his down the toilet!" Rob yelled, bursting into the kitchen. "And I want it back!"

Liz turned to her furious son, grateful for the interruption. She knew she couldn't keep postponing the decision to have another child. It wasn't enough simply to have faced her real reasons for hesitating. Until she was totally honest with John, as well as with herself, she wouldn't have the marriage she wanted.

"Tell you what, Rob," Liz calmed him. "How about if I buy a laundry marking pen today, and tonight you can write your name on all your ties?"

"Really?" His dark eyes gleamed, and Liz hastened to add, "Only where it doesn't show."

"Oh." His face fell.

"Come on, I've got lots of ties in my room. You can pick out any one you want."

"Okay." Rob took her hand. "I'll take the best one, and that'll show that dumb old Jaimie."

"Don't call your brother names," Liz automatically intoned.

"Yes?" Liz absently answered the phone, her mind engrossed in the cookie recipe she was following. "Who?" she frowned as she tried to place the name of her caller.

"Mr. Fawlet," the woman repeated in a rattled tone. "My lawyer. I mean your doctor. Oh . . ." Her young voice rose in despair.

"Take it easy," Liz suggested, "and let's try it again. You are calling Dr. Langdon on behalf of Mr. Fawlet, his lawyer?"

"That's it!" The girl sighed in relief. "I'm just a temporary, and I'm the only one in the office today, and I'm having a terrible time."

"That's too bad," Liz commiserated as she waited for the young woman to get to the message.

"Now"—the girl drew a deep breath and tried again—"Mr. Fawlet said to tell your husband that he's tied up all the loose ends, and he has a court date set for ten-thirty the morning of November fourteenth. Have you got that?"

"Ten-thirty, November fourteenth," Liz parroted before she hung up the phone.

Tied up what loose ends? And what on earth was John going to court for? And why on his birthday?

Or was that particular date simply a coincidence? What could it all be about? She started the mixer again. Her imagination ran riot as she considered possible explanations—from John's having run afoul of the law to his being sued for malpractice—but none of them made any sense. Anything of that nature would have very quickly become common knowledge in the medical community, and someone would have told her.

So what on earth was this all about? Briefly her mind flipped through her book, which had proved so helpful, but this time she drew a total blank. Apparently there was one subject on which the author failed to claim expertise.

To hell with the subtle approach. Liz dumped the eggs into the mixer. If ever a situation called for a frank discussion, this was it. The minute John got home, she was going to demand to know what was going on.

Unfortunately for Liz's nerves, John was very late. He'd called from the hospital to tell her not to hold up dinner for him and that he hoped to be home by ten. However, it was closer to eleven by the time Liz heard his car in the driveway.

She hastily tossed aside the book she'd been trying to read and went to pour him a drink. She met him as he came through the kitchen door, and for a moment her perplexity over Fawlet's cryptic message was eclipsed by concern as she studied the grayish tinge to his lined face. He looked so tired. Tired unto death. The phrase flitted through her mind, and a wave of anxiety and tenderness washed over her.

"I love you, John Langdon." She offered the words like a gift, and a tired smile lifted the corners of his mouth.

"Here." She handed him his drink. "You look as if you could use this."

"Thanks." He took the glass in one hand and used the other to encircle her shoulders and give her a quick squeeze.

"Come in and sit down." Liz urged him toward the family room, feeling vaguely guilty as she did so. He needed to get to bed, but she had to talk to him. And if she didn't do it now, who knew when she'd get another chance? He'd leave early in the morning tomorrow, and, despite his plan to take her out to dinner, she was perfectly aware that the odds of their actually going were less than fifty-fifty.

Liz watched him sink into the leather recliner. "John?" she began hesitantly.

"Sit down." He pulled her into his lap. "Tonight I'm so tired I doubt you'd get a reaction even if you did a repeat of your famous bikini act."

"Infamous, you mean," Liz giggled.

"Whatever. What I need right now is to feel you warm and alive and mine. Especially mine."

Not the words of a man bent on some nefarious purpose, Liz thought as she snuggled into his lap. She sighed with undisguised pleasure at the feel of his oh-so-masculine body beneath hers. John might be too tired, but she wasn't. She snuggled her face into his white shirt, her nose wrinkling at the faint antiseptic odor that clung to it. Her fingers unbuttoned his vest in an attempt to make him more comfortable.

John pulled her closer to his chest with his right arm and then leaned his head back against the soft leather chair.

"John?" Liz tried again.

"Liz?" he gently mocked her. "Now that we've got

the names straightened out, suppose we get down to what's bothering you."

"Why do you think something is bothering me?" she stalled.

"Because you're all fidgety. What happened? Did the boys get us excommunicated?"

Giving up trying to gently lead into the subject, she blurted out, "Your lawyer called today."

"Our lawyer," he casually corrected her, but Liz felt the tension that tautened his body at her words. Her heart sank. He hadn't wanted her to know.

"I'm not interested in semantics," she snapped. "I want to know what he meant."

"Since I don't know what he said..." John sipped his drink.

"He said that the loose ends had all been tied up and that you had a court date for November fourteenth."

"Thank you."

"Thank you! That's all you intend to say? Thank you?" Liz was outraged. "If you think I'm going to let a message like that slide by with a 'thank you'..." She sputtered to a halt.

"Liz," he groaned, "not now. I'm tired."

"And I'm worried!"

"About what?" He opened his eyes and stared at her in surprise.

"About why you suddenly need a lawyer. About whether it has anything to do with me. About..." Her voice trailed off when she saw the anger in his eyes.

"You idiot!" His clipped tones were anything but loverlike. "After fifteen years, you still haven't managed to figure out that I'd cheerfully lie down and die for you?"

"And what do I want with a dead body?" Liz wailed. "I want a husband, preferably one who's around sometimes."

John drained the rest of his drink and set the empty glass down on the end table.

"Liz, I know we have to talk. That's why I wanted to take you out to dinner tomorrow night. To give you a chance to discuss this."

"That's fine, providing you don't get called out on an emergency."

"All right," John gave in. "There's nothing sinister about Fawlet's message. It has to do with my grandfather's trust fund."

"The grandfather who raised you after your parents were killed?"

"Uh-huh. He died when I was a freshman at Cornell, and he wrote his will so all my undergraduate expenses would be paid. The rest of the estate was to be put into a trust, which I would inherit on my fortieth birthday. He believed that too much money too early in life had destroyed my father's initiative, and he wanted to make sure that didn't happen to me. And while it isn't a fortune, the interest from it will more than make up the difference."

Liz jerked up and stared into his face. "Do you mean to tell me that while we were starving our way through med school, there was money available to pay for it?" she demanded furiously.

"And quite a bit more. My great-grandfather was a good friend of George Eastman, and he bought quite a bit of his stock."

Liz was silent for a minute while she digested this totally unexpected information. Finally she asked, "Why didn't you tell me?"

"Guilt, embarrassment. Who knows?" John shrugged. "I felt awful that you were working like a galley slave to keep me in school when I wanted to give you everything. And then, too, in the beginning, I hoped to overturn the will. But the judge ruled that it wasn't capricious, merely shortsighted of my grandfather not to take into consideration the fact that I might want an advanced degree. But shortsightedness is not sufficient grounds for invalidating a will."

"Of all..." Liz paused as his earlier words penetrated her anger at John's grandfather's ill-advised actions. "Make up what difference?"

"Yes..." John drew the word out. "That's what I wanted to talk to you about." He paused.

"So talk," Liz urged him.

"This is actually something that's been in my mind for a long time." He paused and frowned at the ceiling as if searching for the right words. "I really think I could do more good and in the long run reach more patients if I assumed a different role."

"How so?"

"First, there's my research. It's reached the point where it's demanding more time than I have to give to it, and the potential benefits from it are tremendous. Then that course I taught last year at the med school clarified something in my mind. The proper training of young pediatricians is absolutely vital. They need to learn much more than simple facts. It's essential that they be taught how to relate to their patients as small human beings with identities all their own instead of seeing them as a series of diseases. And of equal importance, they need to learn to appreciate how parents' attitudes can affect their children. Far too many medical students simply dismiss the parents as none of their concern. I feel that by helping to train tomorrow's pediatricians, I can make a much greater and more lasting contribution than I am now."

"That makes sense." Liz nodded, an incredible elation filling her. Teaching would also have the added benefit of drastically reducing his working hours.

Having no trouble following her line of thought, he added, "I don't like the fact that I'm never at home any more than you do, and I've always wanted to have more time for the twins."

And any other children they might have. The thought fluttered through her mind, and she glanced up into John's watchful face. He was being honest with her. It was imperative that she tell him the truth, even if it didn't make her look very good.

"Uh, John?" She began to fiddle with the top button of his vest.

"You don't like the idea?" He sounded unsure of himself.

"I love it," she hastened to assure him. "It's not that. It's about... It was something Carol said in Washington."

"And what did Carol say?"

"It serves him right," she blurted out.

"It serves him right?" John sounded confused.

"Uh-huh. You know how every once in a while somebody says something, and all kinds of things suddenly fall into place?"

"Yes." He nodded encouragingly.

"Well..." Liz gave the abused button another twist, then stared in surprise as it came off in her hand. "We were talking about children, and I suddenly realized I was trying to use another child as a bargaining point to get you to lighten your work load."

She risked a glance up into his impassive face. "As dumb as it sounds, I'd never realized it before. I really believed what I was saying about being afraid to try again."

"Don't be too hard on yourself, Liz." John's strong fingers speared through her curls, and he cradled her head against his chest.

"You aren't mad?" she asked hesitantly.

"You aren't the only one whose motives didn't bear too close a scrutiny," he said dryly. "Oh, I wanted more children all right, but I also wanted to bind you to me with as many bonds as possible. You tried to hide your unhappiness, but I knew how much you hated my long hours, and in the back of my mind I was always afraid you might decide to leave."

"What?" Liz bounced up, not even noticing when his fingers tugged her curls. "My God, John, don't you know I love you to distraction?"

"My distraction," he chuckled, the uncertain look she hated fading. "You really threw me when you frizzed up your hair," he confessed.

"Permed," Liz giggled. "Never tell a lady her hair is frizzy. Besides, I did it all for your benefit. I bought a book on how to rejuvenate our marriage, and it said I should update my image."

"You leave your image alone." John pulled her back against him. "It feels lovely just the way it is." His hand brushed lightly over her breasts, and she shivered. "Although," he continued thoughtfully, "I rather liked the plastic wrap bikini, and that massage in the bathtub . . ." His voice trailed away in remembered bliss.

"Just wait. I haven't even made it all the way through the book yet, and"—her voice dropped conspiratorially—"I hear the author is writing a sequel."

"I live in hope." John slipped a hand under her chin and pressed a hard kiss onto her lips.

"Are you going to look for a teaching job, then?" She waited for his reply with a thudding heart. When it came, it seemed like the answer to years of prayer.

"I've already been offered one. I was going to tell you tomorrow night over a romantic candlelit dinner."

"I'd rather be told over kisses any day." She arched her body into his.

"Don't you want to know where we're going to live?"

"Not particularly." She began to run the tip of her tongue over the stubble on his chin. A shiver chased down her spine at the sensation. "As long as we're together, I don't care where we live."

"God, I love you!" He pulled her willing body to him and fastened his mouth on hers. Finally he eased her flushed face back into his shoulder and said, "Boston."

"Boston who?" she muttered.

"Boston where. I've been offered a professorship at Harvard." The pride in his voice was unmistakable.

"Harvard!" Liz was suitably impressed. "Harvard Med School? Wait a minute." She suddenly remembered something. "Harvard's in Cambridge, isn't it?" She jackknifed up, her euphoria shattered.

"Uh-huh."

"Those two men you invited to our hotel room for

drinks. Santa Claus and the gimlet-eyed psychiatrist . . ."

"From the university's selection committee. I'd been corresponding with them for almost six months. I didn't say anything to you about it because I didn't want you to be disappointed if they didn't want me. As it turned out, they made the formal offer the next morning."

"Oh." Liz subsided against him. "Did you explain why I behaved so strangely?"

"Of course not! You're perfectly free to behave any way you want. If they don't like it, that's their problem. Actually though, I think Santa Claus figured out what the crackling was."

"Not the psychiatrist?" Liz groaned, feeling like an idiot.

John laughed. "No, I think Irving was too busy trying to find a deep, hidden motive to notice the obvious one."

"So when do we go?" Liz asked.

"About the first of the year. That should give me time to transfer my practice to another doctor. I thought we'd take the boys and fly to Boston this weekend to look for a house."

"A big house." Liz gave him an impish grin.

"Big?"

"At least five bedrooms. That way if we get twins again, we'll have someplace to put them."

John captured her head between his hands and studied her ecstatic features intently. "I was wrong," he said finally.

"About what?"

"I'm not too tired." He grinned. "Let's go upstairs

and try out whatever your author suggested in the last chapter you read."

He set her on her feet and held out his hand. Liz placed her own in his and smiled tremulously.

All this and heaven too. The old refrain echoed through her mind as she went with him.

WONDERFUL ROMANCE NEWS:

Do you know about the exciting SECOND CHANCE AT LOVE/TO HAVE AND TO HOLD newsletter? Are you on our *free* mailing list? If reading all about your favorite authors, getting sneak previews of their latest releases, and being filled in on all the latest happenings and events in the romance world sound good to you, then you'll love our SECOND CHANCE AT LOVE and TO HAVE AND TO HOLD Romance News.

If you'd like to be added to our mailing list, just fill out the coupon below and send it in…and we'll send you your *free* newsletter every three months — hot off the press.

☐ *Yes, I would like to receive your free SECOND CHANCE AT LOVE/TO HAVE AND TO HOLD newsletter.*

Name _____

Address _____

City _____ State/Zip _____

Please return this coupon to:

    Berkley Publishing
    200 Madison Avenue, New York, New York 10016
    Att: Rebecca Kaufman

HERE'S WHAT READERS ARE SAYING ABOUT

To Have and to Hold

"Your TO HAVE AND TO HOLD series is a fabulous and long overdue idea."
— *A. D., Upper Darby, PA**

"I have been reading romance novels for over ten years and feel the TO HAVE AND TO HOLD series is the best I have read. It's exciting, sensitive, refreshing, well written. Many thanks for a series of books I can relate to."
— *O. K., Bensalem, PA**

"I enjoy your books tremendously."
— *J. C., Houston, TX**

"I love the books and read them over and over."
— *E. K., Warren, MI**

"You have another winner with the new TO HAVE AND TO HOLD series."
— *R. P., Lincoln Park, MI**

"I love the new series TO HAVE AND TO HOLD."
— *M. L., Cleveland, OH**

"I've never written a fan letter before, but TO HAVE AND TO HOLD is fantastic."
— *E. S., Narberth, PA**

*Name and address available upon request

Second Chance at Love

____ 07812-3	SOMETIMES A LADY #196	Jocelyn Day
____ 07813-1	COUNTRY PLEASURES #197	Lauren Fox
____ 07814-X	TOO CLOSE FOR COMFORT #198	Liz Grady
____ 07815-8	KISSES INCOGNITO #199	Christa Merlin
____ 07816-6	HEAD OVER HEELS #200	Nicola Andrews
____ 07817-4	BRIEF ENCHANTMENT #201	Susanna Collins
____ 07818-2	INTO THE WHIRLWIND #202	Laurel Blake
____ 07819-0	HEAVEN ON EARTH #203	Mary Haskell
____ 07820-4	BELOVED ADVERSARY #204	Thea Frederick
____ 07821-2	SEASWEPT #205	Maureen Norris
____ 07822-0	WANTON WAYS #206	Katherine Granger
____ 07823-9	A TEMPTING MAGIC #207	Judith Yates
____ 07956-1	HEART IN HIDING #208	Francine Rivers
____ 07957-X	DREAMS OF GOLD AND AMBER #209	Robin Lynn
____ 07958-8	TOUCH OF MOONLIGHT #210	Liz Grady
____ 07959-6	ONE MORE TOMORROW #211	Aimée Duvall
____ 07960-X	SILKEN LONGINGS #212	Sharon Francis
____ 07961-8	BLACK LACE AND PEARLS #213	Elissa Curry
____ 08070-5	SWEET SPLENDOR #214	Diana Mars
____ 08071-3	BREAKFAST WITH TIFFANY #215	Kate Nevins
____ 08072-1	PILLOW TALK #216	Lee Williams
____ 08073-X	WINNING WAYS #217	Christina Dair
____ 08074-8	RULES OF THE GAME #218	Nicola Andrews
____ 08075-6	ENCORE #219	Carole Buck
____ 08115-9	SILVER AND SPICE #220	Jeanne Grant
____ 08116-7	WILDCATTER'S KISS #221	Kelly Adams
____ 08117-5	MADE IN HEAVEN #222	Linda Raye
____ 08118-3	MYSTIQUE #223	Ann Cristy
____ 08119-1	BEWITCHED #224	Linda Barlow
____ 08120-5	SUDDENLY THE MAGIC #225	Karen Keast

All of the above titles are $1.95
Prices may be slightly higher in Canada.

Available at your local bookstore or return this form to:

SECOND CHANCE AT LOVE
Book Mailing Service
P.O. Box 690, Rockville Centre, NY 11571

Please send me the titles checked above. I enclose _____ Include 75¢ for postage and handling if one book is ordered; 25¢ per book for two or more not to exceed $1.75. California, Illinois, New York and Tennessee residents please add sales tax.

NAME_____

ADDRESS_____

CITY_____STATE/ZIP_____

(allow six weeks for delivery)   SK-41b

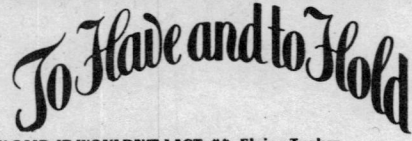